DEAD MEN SINGING:

THE MEN WHO FOUGHT FOR TEXAS

H. BEDFORD-JONES

DEAD MEN SINGING:

THE MEN WHO
FOUGHT FOR TEXAS

H. BEDFORD-JONES

INTERIOR ILLUSTRATIONS BY

R. FARRINGTON ELWELL

ALTUS PRESS • 2015

© 2015 Altus Press • First Edition—2015

EDITED AND DESIGNED BY
Matthew Moring

PUBLISHING HISTORY
"The Buffalo Hunter" originally appeared in the August 10, 1935 issue of *Short Stories* magazine (Vol. 152 No. 3).

"The Seventh Child" originally appeared in the September 10, 1935 issue of *Short Stories* magazine (Vol. 152 No. 5).

"The Jailbird" originally appeared in the September 25, 1935 issue of *Short Stories* magazine (Vol. 152 No. 6).

"The Rifleman" originally appeared in the October 25, 1935 issue of *Short Stories* magazine (Vol. 153 No. 2).

"Loser Pays" originally appeared in the January 25, 1936 issue of *Short Stories* magazine (Vol. 154 No. 2).

"The Man Alone" originally appeared in the February 25, 1936 issue of *Short Stories* magazine (Vol. 154 No. 4).

THANKS TO
Everard P. Digges LaTouche and Gerd Pircher

TABLE OF CONTENTS

I

THE BUFFALO HUNTER

A cold, blowing night in Texas, near the Guadeloupe River. Dawn was threatening the pale stars. A strange singing sound reached me, yet for miles around was no human presence. Startled, incredulous, I listened.

Again and again, now fainter, now clearer, drifted the sound of voices. It came from nowhere, from everywhere; from the thin clouds, from the chaparral, from the very ground. Then suddenly the lilt grew upon me, the words became distinct, as though the singer were passing close by me but invisible:

"We were hunters and politicians, soldiers, half-breeds and scouts,
Preachers and clerks and gentry, gamblers and country louts,
Lawyers and ciboleros, wandering to and fro—
And by God, sir, we fought for Texas a hundred years ago!"

And then—I could have sworn to it—through the darkness from nowhere came a burst of rough, ribald, bawdy voices swelling and dying away again down the night upon a rush of ghostly hoof beats:

"Here's to you, Cibolero, damn your eyes!"

Cibolero? The swing of the word fascinated me. What did it mean? What were these voices from the prairie? True, the Texan war for freedom had started close by here at Gonzales, in 1835, a hundred years ago.

THE CIBOLERO reined in his shaggy horse, alert for a repetition of the laugh. He was a rangy, thin-faced, bearded man, very brown, clad in ragged buckskin. His Comanche moccasins rasped in the wooden clogs of his Spanish stirrups. He held a long rifle poised across his saddlehorn, poised and cocked, ready.

The harsh laugh came again. Then a hideous, unspeakable scream that drove across the sunlight to chill the very blood.

Somewhere below lay the waterhole, invisible. Here the naked rocks blazed with heat. The entire Puercos Valley shimmered and danced with heat waves, clear to the hot blue mountains. The downpour of sunlight was parching, furious, intolerable.

"All right, stranger!" rose a voice. "Water up and welcome, but keep that rifle low. You're covered."

The Cibolero let his eager horse go on down the steep descent. The trail turned very sharply. The waterhole came into sight, twenty feet distant. The Cibolero halted dead, as another harsh laugh greeted him, and the scene.

"Bet ye never heard a 'Pache holler afore! Well, this 'un did."

The Cibolero stared at a short, squat man of forty, wearing stained buckskin and an enormous sombrero wound with tarnished silver braid. Muttonchop whiskers, Mexican style, and small shrewd eyes flanked a huge hooked nose.

At this man's feet lay a bound and naked Indian, still quivering, as a snake quivers long after life is extinct. At one side were two dead horses and an old, rickety wagon, and against the wheels lay four dead bodies—Mexicans, perhaps pulque hunters. Two men, a woman, a young girl, all naked and dead. The men were much cut up; Apache raiders believed in removing the source of future generations.

The squat white man obviously cherished the same belief. As he held up his red knife and chuckled, the Cibolero felt a little sick.

"Yeah, he hollered when I give him his own med'cine. This was the only one of the three we didn't down first crack; we let him set for a spell, and by gosh, it got his nerve! Ye see, three 'Paches had jumped these here folks, then we jumped the

'Paches. Well, stranger, light and water up. Seen you coming for quite a spell, and Red Sky figured you for a white man. Kirker is the name, Jim Kirker."

The Cibolero dismounted and gave his name.

"Nathan Jackson?" Kirker repeated. "Why, say! You're the feller they call the Cibolero—the buffler hunter! Proud to grip your claw. Come on out, Red Sky; no need to worry about him. The Cibolero, huh? Thought you was up around Santy Fé?

WITH A nod, the Cibolero followed his horse to the water, and after a drink made unhurried response.

"Yeah. I'm headin' down into Texas to see some friends o' mine."

"Just come from Bexar myself. There's hell to pay in them parts." Kirker stooped and deftly removed the scalp of the dead Apache. Another figure emerged from among the rocks; it was that of a lithe, pock-marked Indian, to whom Kirker jerked his thumb.

"Say, Cibolero, shake hands with Red Sky. Delaware from York State. Him and me are in business. If it goes good, we'll ketch in more of his folks."

"Business?" the Cibolero repeated, puzzled. Kirker nodded, and going to one of the dead Mexicans, removed the scalp and regarded it critically. Then he grinned.

"This ain't so bad; can't tell it from 'Pache hair noways, if ye lift it right. I dunno about the gal, there; the hair's too soft, maybe. Red Sky, trim up the woman's pelt a bit, and mind your eye."

"What in the devil's name are you about?" the Cibolero demanded.

"Making money. I seen Gin'ral Cos down to Bexar; him and me are friendly. I'll get a reg'lar contract out of Santy Anny for 'Pache scalps—hundred dollars per each. The joke of it is," and Kirker grinned, "they can't tell Mexican from 'Pache scalps! So me and Red Sky will profit. Ye see, I got in trouble over to Chihuahua; the governor there put a bounty of nine thousand dollars on my head. Ain't that a brag? Well, Cos has fixed things up. I ain't a outlaw no more and everything's fine. Where you heading for?"

"Gonzales."

"Huh! I reckon you know them Texians are out to raise Cain?"

The Cibolero shook his head. From his pouch he took a strip of jerked meat and began to chew at it.

"Nope. Santa Fé is a long ways from San Antonio."

"Bexar, you mean. The mission's San Antonio, and the town is Bexar. Ain't you heard that Santy Anny is military dictator of Mexico?"

"Yes. That's no news."

The two men fell into talk, and the Cibolero, for the first time, began to comprehend what sort of trouble was going on here in the State of Texas, which was now largely settled by Americans, frontiersmen who lived by the rifle. Entire colonies had come in, formed by Austin and others, to take up Texas land. Texas was now a state, governed by its own representatives down at Coahuila—or had been until Santa Anna became dictator.

Santa Anna had abolished the state legislatures and the constitution of republican Mexico; as dictator, he was supreme. He had crushed all opposition with savage hand. The Texians alone were in resistance, which thus far had been passive, to his program. And the attention of Santa Anna was now turned to them.

His brother-in-law, General Cos, had come to San Antonio with strong forces and was proceeding to disarm all citizens in Texas. The representatives at Coahuila had been flung into prison, such of them as did not escape. Delegates from all over Texas had met at San Felipe to form a new state constitution, within the republic of Mexico, demanding that Santa Anna recognize it. His reply was to jail those who brought him the message, and to issue imperative orders to General Cos.

"And them Texians," observed Kirker, "they holler that they ain't going to be disarmed, and they mean it. Likewise, them greasers mean business."

THIS WAS the most ominous thing; the Mexicans did mean business. Their troops and artillery held Texas powerless. Their possession of San Antonio de Bexar, the one large city in the state, gave them a base of action. The half-organized settlers had no troops and no money. Some, like Sam Houston, were all for cutting loose from Mexico and forming their own republic, but the masses were awed by the idea of fighting a disciplined power, as well they might be.

"They sure are a-getting their mad up, though," said Kirker, chuckling. "Dragoons are being sent out all over the country, gathering in rifles and so forth, and having trouble doing it. I hear that land is being grabbed, too, which looks bad. If there's any real war started, these here Texians get wiped clean, right down to the cradle. Santy Anny aims to kill off all foreigners that disagree with him. So steer clear of sojers."

"I'm not looking for trouble," the Cibolero said. "I want to find some folks I know. You don't reckon any real war will start?"

"Sure to start. Me, I ain't no Texian. It's no skin off my nose if them settlers gets too brash and are wiped out. I got my own affairs and stick to 'em."

"Hm! I guess that's sensible. Did you happen to hear anything about a family named Sisson? From Pike County, Missouri? Last I heard, they were heading for Gonzales to take up land near there."

"Nope. There's a sight o' folks in Texas, and I ain't met only half. What about a horn of liquor? I got a jug of prime stuff cached with our horses."

"No, thanks; I must move on." The Cibolero drank again, filled his water bottle, and gave his horse a last short drink. After all, he reflected aloud, the settlers would have too much sense to provoke the wrath of Mexico. With this, Kirker disagreed.

"Seems like they're all politicians, Cibolero, on one side; and on t'other, crazy galoots spoiling for a fight. Like that feller Jim Bowie. I tell you, them Texians are right quick to take up a' scrap, somehow! Them that ain't politicians, of course. Well, luck to you! And mind your step, too, if you meet any sojers."

The Cibolero nodded and mounted. As he rode off, he turned for a last look at the waterhole. The two men there were spreading their trophies in the sun to dry.

HEADING STRAIGHT for Gonzales through the wilderness, the Cibolero rode on, day after day, keeping well to the north of Bexar, as San Antonio was generally known. Gradually the desert and mountains and naked rocks fell beyond the horizon; slowly the lush river country of grazing herds and settlements opened ahead. But as he rode, the Cibolero grew more and more uneasy.

He did not like the new day that had come to Mexico with Santa Anna; a hard, ruthless, lecherous man who had done great things for himself. Gone were the old courtly Spanish customs, the friendly intercourse with Yankees; a new breed had come into power. And thinking of Jenny Sisson as he rode, now and again fumbling at the paper packet sewn inside his buckskin shirt, the Cibolero frowned and worried.

On a day, he came out abruptly upon a new settlement north of Gonzales, a cluster of cabins whose bark was still green. A lean brown hunter, in tattered clothes and coonskin cap, was perched on a stump, waving his arms and yelling excitedly, while a whiskey jug went around the circle of listeners. The Cibolero could hear his voice from afar.

"What's it mean? No gov'ment without representation, I tell ye! Us Texians has got to stand up for our rights! Us Texians—"

"Hey, Dick!" shouted someone. "Since when was you a Texian, you N'awleens 'gator?"

The brown man whirled savagely. "Since when? Since I seen them two Brown boys shot down, over ort the Nueces River— shot and then ripped with lances. And for why? Wouldn't give up their rifles, that's why! And if you'd heerd the gal screaming from the cabin, too, it'd ha' been enough. Right then, by God, I become a Texian and I stays a Texian! And if you boys don't tote your guns down to Gonzales—"

He broke off suddenly, as the Cibolero came riding up. The voices ceased. Men turned and stared; women peered from cabin doorways. Eyes and faces were suspicious, questioning, alert. One could never be sure nowadays. The Cibolero drew rein.

"Howdy, folks." At the homely words, all tension relaxed. The Cibolero swung out of the saddle, leaned his rifle against a stump, and stretched. "By gosh, I come all the way from Santa Fé, boys. Got a drink to spare?"

Already they were surrounding him eagerly, aflame with curiosity. From Santa Fé, that unknown, distant city of song and story! The Cibolero expertly swung the jug on his elbow and lifted it to his lips. Presently he handed it back.

"Prime stuff; obliged to you. What's all this talk about trouble?"

A MOMENTARY silence. Then the agitator spoke up.

"What? You mean to say as you don't' know about it?"

"Santa Fé is a long ways," and the Cibolero smiled. "I reckon I'm a lot ignorant, folks. Say, did any of you ever meet up with some Pike County settlers by the name of Sisson? Last I heard they were headed for Gonzales—"

"What?" broke in the speaker eagerly. "Pete Sisson and his old woman, and the two gals? Why, I stayed two days with them folks! They're a spell out of Gonzales on the crick road. Sisson, he's got the rheumatiz bad; he's all crippled up. And that oldest gal, Jenny—maybe you're the feller she was allus talking about? The buffler hunter?"

"Reckon I am, mister; I usually go by the name of the Cibolero. I've come a right smart ways to see them folks, too."

"Hurray! That gal allowed you'd join up, if you was here!" The agitator was upon him, breathless, pouring forth excited words.

"Listen here! That goddam Gin'ral Cos, he's a-sending sojers, a hull passel of 'em, up to Gonzales. They figure to grab everybody's rifles, and the old brass cannon they've got at Gonzales too—"

"Hold on, this is all new to me," exclaimed the Cibolero. "What for are the guns being grabbed?"

"What for? Tyranny, by God!" With a scream, the brown man leaped back to his stump. "That's what I'm a-telling you folks—tyranny! We got a right to bear arms. It's in the Consitution back home. Us Texians have got it in our state constitution here, but now that's all smashed to hell. There ain't no more state gov'ment, hear me? Just Santy Anny. They're taking our guns everywhere. They put Steve Austin in jail—yeah, Austin hisself! They got us Texians in jail all over, they're a-grabbing farms and saying land titles ain't no good, and we got to fight!"

"We can handle any greasers that come this way," said a skeptical settler.

"Yah! You boys set on your hunkers and say it ain't your business," yelled the brown man. "By God, it'll be your business when them lancers come this way, you bet; first you know, you got a lance in your belly! And you women folks in there, you'd better light a shuck for the woods when them dragoons show up—by God, you had! None of your business, huh? None of Davy Crockett's business, neither, but he's on the way—"

"What's that?" shouted somebody "Colonel Crockett from Tennessee?"

"Himself, and a many more like him. I tell you, hell's blazing down to Gonzales! There's a new gov'ment being set up to San Felipe, and we got powder and guns coming in from N'awleens—"

The uproar rose again. The Cibolero went to one of the cabins, obtained a cornpone and a strip of side meat from a woman, and listened while he ate, with a mental shrug. It was none of his business, as a matter of fact. He was not a Texian. The names spouted by this agitator meant nothing to him. Jim Bowie, Travis, Austin—these men, proscribed by the new

Mexican government, were unknown to him. His only Texas interest was the girl Jenny from Pike County. At thought of her, he touched the packet under his shirt, and a smile crept into his eyes.

He had nothing against the Mexicans; up in Santa Fé, he had many friends among them. Not that he blamed these excited, blaring Texians for sticking by their guns and resenting oppression; but he was like Jim Kirker. It was no skin off his nose what happened in these parts. These fellows had settled in Mexico with their eyes open. So many of them had settled here in Texas, indeed, that they had pretty well crowded out the Mexicans.

As to atrocities, he judged that the stump orator was full of whiskey and exaggeration. "See you in Gonzales!" he sang out, when he mounted and rode on. A chorus of voices made response, and rifles were brandished; they were getting worked up, all right.

THAT NIGHT he ran into a one-man camp. A traveler was roasting a wild turkey over a tiny fire, and hailed the Cibolero delightedly. A wandering preacher, this, who had left his Bible in Nacogdoches and was carrying powder—in his saddlebags, his pockets, hung to his belt, stuffed everywhere.

"So you never heard o' Sam Houston?" observed the preacher, as they talked. "Well, just wait! Down to San Felipe, where them aristocrats are settled, they got a gov'ment all ready. Houston, he writ the constitution; he's all for secession from Mexico, but that's too much for most folks to swallow. Now that they're calling it treason to have rifles, I dunno. I hear the Mexicans are grabbing farms and land, too."

He shook his head at the Cibolero's frowning question.

"Killing? I dunno. I'm a-heading for Gonzales. I hear Gin'ral Cos has sent an army to disarm the folks there. They got an old brass cannon, a four-pounder, to use against the Comanches, and Cos aims to get it. Texian? You bet I'm a Texian. Come from Kaintuck three months ago. Ain't you waiting the night?"

The Cibolero was not waiting. After an hour's sleep he mounted and rode on; he was growing more uneasy about Jenny and her folks. It did look as though some fire underlay all this smoke. A preacher toting powder—that was funny. Talk about conventions and politics meant little to him; it looked like these settlers had all gone crazy.

He rode hard, careless now whether his horse lasted or not. He came into Gonzales of an evening, worn out, starving, his horse exhausted. To his amazement he found the little town of straggling log cabins and adobe huts in a blaze of light from bonfires, aflame with voices and excitement. He had anticipated seeing hundreds of settlers gathered here, but he found only a few dozen.

Someone caught him as he half fell from his horse. It was Deaf Smith, a scout whom he had met in the Western country, and who greeted him vociferously.

"Hey, Cibolero! Here's a jug; drink hearty. Just in time, you old grizzly! Them sojers is camped acrost the crick. Hey, everybody! Here's a Texian for you—come all the way from Santy Fé to get in the scrap!"

Men gathered excitedly. The Cibolero drank, and the liquor set him on fire. War? Yes; the brass cannon was ready, the Mexican soldiers were here, the morrow would see fighting! Voices roared on every side. Beneath the wild exuberance lay a deeper note; these men were scouts, settlers, Indian fighters, not mere talkers. Their excitement was backed by a grim purpose. Disarm? Not a bit of it!

More drinks, and a bite to eat. The Cibolero felt himself swept along with the tumultuous stream; he was amazed to hear of what had happened in Texas lately, of how the whole people were taking arms. War? It was a certainty. None the less, he pursued inquiries about the Sisson family and found several who knew them well.

Yes, old Pete Sisson was bedridden. He and his folks had not come into town. He was friendly with the greasers anyhow. The

Cibolero got a description of their place and the way thither well fixed in his mind, then let it all wait. He was done up, the liquor was good, the Sissons were safe—and here was fighting on the morrow. He must stay and see what happened. Mexican faces, too. He was newly astonished at how many Mexicans sided with the Texians. It was all a muddle to him. By midnight, however, human endurance had reached its end. He was snoring fast and hard, the world forgotten.

SUNLIGHT WAKENED him, and a wild outburst of voices. He sat up, reached for his rifle.

"Pile out, pile out, everybody!" came the shouts. "River road, all hands! Hurry!"

The Cibolero staggered out into the sunlight. Dust was rising in clouds, men were riding furiously. No time to seek his own horse; he caught the first saddled beast in sight, swung up, and pounded off in the wake of the straggling riders.

There was the river. Across the stream, on an eminence, the Mexicans were camped. The horses splashed through at the ford. Voices rose; a parley had taken place. A screen of oak trees shut off everything ahead. Now Deaf Smith appeared, shouting at the men. Some dismounted and went crashing ahead on foot to where the little brass cannon was placed. The Cibolero found himself turned to the left, with a number of other mounted men.

The open ground came suddenly in sight, and sudden startled silence fell. The breeze blew the dust away. A bugle was shrilling, the enemy were in sight; lines of cavalry drawn up, lance-points a-glitter in the sun, blue and red uniforms, brass dragoon helmets, gold-laced officers. Carbines, discipline, against a ragged line of riflemen.

Deliberately, the Cibolero left his weapon unloaded. It was not his fight; he was here to look on. He heard voices all around; treason, no quarter promised, the cannon was ready. Everything was a muddle to the Cibolero. He stared, realized suddenly that the lines of cavalry were wheeling to bugle calls, were on the point of charging.

Then—crash! The brass cannon roared out. A wild yell rang down the Texian line. Men leaped from cover and started across the open, madly charging the lines of cavalry. Rifles began to speak, the explosions running to right and left. Powder smoke hid everything. The bewildered Cibolero could see little until the dust and smoke thinned. Then amazement seized him. Wild yells pealed up, yells of triumph, of ferocity, of exultation.

Those disciplined ranks were gone, shattered, blown like leaves on the wind. Men and horses lay rolling or kicking. The officers had turned tail, the dispersed dragoons were in wild flight. With sudden relief from their tremendous tension, the Texians burst into cheers, oaths, hysterical laughter. Somebody pounded the Cibolero on the back.

"Licked 'em! What'd I tell you? One Texian can lick ten yeller-bellies any day! Smashed 'em with one volley—look at 'em run!"

Someone yelled something about Lexington; others took up the word, for these men had not forgotten the Revolution. Licked them! Texians could stand up to the boasted cavalry of Mexico and lick them all at one volley! The thing was proven at last.

CONFUSED, THE CIBOLERO finally found his way out of the frenzied scene. There would be no more fighting; the fun was over. The Cibolero climbed aboard the first horse he saw and went riding away. It was all over now; he could go and find Jenny at last. He was so filled with this thought, that he paid little heed to the horse, until he realized with many a curse that it was an old, slow, jaded beast. However, no matter! A new eagerness had replaced the thrill and quick excitement of the battle in his heart, and his eyes were alight.

Jenny and her younger sister, their ma, old Pete Sisson, all waiting for him! He had a present for Jenny safely sewed inside his shirt, and his fingers sought it anew. A lace scarf that had come from Mexico City. No doubt stained with sweat and dirt by this time, but it would wash. And how her pretty face would beam at sight of it! Almost seventeen was Jenny, and high time she was married.

"And she will be now, quick enough!" muttered the Cibolero happily. "I'll jerk her out of all this mess. No Texas for me! Just because a bunch o' cavalry gets licked, these Texians think all Mexico is their meat. They ain't got sense enough to know that Santa Anna can throw twenty thousand prime troops at 'em, with cannon to boot. And he'll do it, too. Just like Jim Kirker said. He'll wipe 'em clean."

The sun rose higher, and the skinny old horse shuffled along. The Cibolero, remembering the landmarks given him, made no mistake. After a long time he came into a trail, and saw a lance lying in the dust. An eight-foot lance, the shaft two inches thick, the razor-keen head three inches across. He frowned; riders had come this way, Mexicans! Just as well that he had not fired his rifle. Might have need of it yet.

They'd learn something if they monkeyed with him. A harsh laugh came to his lips. A new contempt for Mexicans had arisen within him; more correctly, a contempt for their fighting ability. There were good fighters in Mexico, yes, but not among these soldiers, the scum of the cities, many of them convicts. Such men disarm the Texians? Not likely. Well, it was not his business. He was no Texian.

A DISTANT patch of green, a line of thick trees; there was the creek. A trickle of smoke was lifting, and he sighed in happy relief. That was the place, all right, and everything was quiet. Cooking dinner, most likely. Jennie's hot-bread would sure be welcome, and a horn of liquor as well. The Cibolero realized all of a sudden how thirsty and hungry he was. Until this moment, he had been too excited and eager to think of it.

Gradually the trees grew nearer. The thicker, denser clump forming a windbreak about the cabin took shape, as the Cibolero rode among the outlying oaks and nut trees. He drew rein, suddenly; he sat listening, wondering. Then he swung to the ground and turned in among the trees, and halted.

What was it, off there to the left? A man's voice, assuredly, cursing and laughing; then came a queer choked, panting gasp. Something was moving over there, crashing among the berry vines.

"Hi!" called the Cibolero gaily. "Hi, Jenny! That you hunting bear—"

A wild, wailing cry came to him in response. A cry that actually froze something within him. From that instant he was a changed man.

A figure came plunging forward, the figure of a girl; no, not Jenny at all, but her sister. Running, mouth wide open for breath, hardly a rag on her body; and behind, thrashing along and swooping to clutch her, a soldier. A Mexican. Now he had caught up with her, and one swiftly choked scream burst from the girl.

The Cibolero had been momentarily paralyzed by all this. He wakened abruptly, let his rifle fall, and forgot it as he flung himself in among the vines. Not until this instant did the other man realize his presence, but it was too late for defense. The Cibolero saw that there was fresh blood on the uniform tunic. He saw nothing else, heard nothing at all, until he found himself standing in the drifted sunlight beneath the trees, with what was left of a man hanging in his hands.

He wakened. He was dimly aware of a thin screaming that had now ceased; this soldier had been crying out. He let the limp thing fall, and his eyes went to the girl, widening in horror. She lay there unconscious on her back, her small breasts heaving above her panting lungs. Upon her face was a smear of blood, though she seemed unhurt.

"Hola, Ramon!" A voice came to him as he stood, a distant laughing voice in Spanish. "Fetch the little one in, hombre! Share and share alike, comrade—"

A shiver seized upon the Cibolero. He swallowed hard, stared down for a moment at the unconscious girl, then his head came up. He turned and strode back to the trail, where he picked up his rifle and primed it. An old Kentucky rifle, this, long and heavy and beautiful; it had been the pride of his life, until now.

FORGETTING HIS jaded horse, the Cibolero struck off along the trail, on foot. He made no effort to hide. The very heart and soul was frozen fast within him, yet his eyes were burning as he strode. Jenny, Jenny! Nothing else mattered.

The clearing grew and fell open before him; in the midst of it was set the log cabin. At one side grazed horses, saddled cavalry horses. Six men were gathered, eating and drinking, at a table under the umbrella tree in front of the cabin. Ma Sisson had always wanted a table under a tree, he remembered.

She would want it no more; that, nor anything else.

A glance showed him everything as he advanced. She lay just outside the doorway, one arm over the breast of Pete Sisson. He had fallen on the threshold, a rifle still clutched in his hand. She must have been cut down as she caught him; a saber must have done that frightful thing. Only an axe or a saber—

And Jenny, Jenny!

The Cibolero halted, and the breath came from his nostrils in a low whistling groan. He saw her white body for the first time in his life; all her sweet body, stretched there at one side, but not all white now. She was limp and dead. He knew the sight of death instantly.

"*Madre de Dios!*" A voice jerked out the startled words as one of the men about the table caught sight of him.

They saw him, all of them, saw him and leaped up; they were crying out, clutching at weapons. The Cibolero's eyes cleared. He said nothing, but lifted the rifle and slowly pressed the trigger. The white smoke spurted.

The Cibolero reversed the rifle and swung it up, as the other five came running at him. No matter if the hot barrel burned his hands; there was a worse burning in his brain. The foremost soldier pitched down to the blow, and the walnut stock of the rifle snapped off short. The Cibolero remembered that a Kentucky rifle always acted this way if clubbed; somebody had told him as much. No matter. He had no more need of it.

The remaining four were upon him. His forgotten knife came out. There was a flash, a play of glittering steel in the sifted sunlight. Under their combined rush, the Cibolero tottered and lost balance, and was borne backward.

But as he fell, his free hand gripped one of those men close and hard.

The dust swirled. A wild sound rose out of the dust, a bubbling scream, as a man flung himself frantically aside. He got to his feet and ran toward the horses; his whole face was split by a slash across the cheeks, and blood dribbled down over his tunic. He got to a horse and after a while clawed his way into the saddle. The other horses followed as he rode away and there was none to stay them.

The other three soldiers lay on the ground with the Cibolero, and tried vainly to flail clear of him. He had flung his long arms about all three, gripping them very tight, and in one body his knife was buried to the hilt; this man did not thrash about for long.

The Cibolero glared into their sweating, pallid features, their bulging eyes. Two of them; no more. He knew that the wounded man had ridden away; he realized it clearly, and was unworried. There was no haste. He would get that man later. Now he was gripping the two living men and the dead man very close, so close they could not use their weapons. Not that he cared a snap about their knives. He felt nothing. He was no longer capable of any bodily feeling. Desperate, they made frantic efforts to get clear of his grip, and could not.

Of a sudden, the Cibolero shifted himself. He moved his body, and flung their whole weight sideways, rolled them over. Swift and agile as a panther, he unexpectedly loosened his hold on them. He got clear, gained his feet on the instant, and was reaching for them as they scrambled up.

From the two men burst hoarse panting words, incoherent oaths, appeals, frenzied cries. They still had their knives.

THE CIBOLERO caught hold of them as they came up, one hand to each slim brown throat, and his fingers sank into the flesh. The third soldier, with the knife still buried in his back, slid away and lay quietly in the dust. The Cibolero stood up to his full height, dragging those two with him, holding each of them by the throat.

They used their knives, but he felt nothing at all. Every sense was dead within him, everything except the one driving urge. His long arms swung the two heads together with a crunch.

One of the soldiers wailed out terribly, though his voice soon died. Again and again the long arms moved them apart and brought them together. Presently, however, the Cibolero realized that they were like limp dolls in his grip. He looked down, his brain cleared, and he let them fall. They sprawled in the dust like two heaps of old reddened rage.

One had got away. He remembered this with a stab of hurt in his brain, and swung around. Once more he caught sight of the white, twisted dead body of Jenny.

The Cibolero put one hand inside his shirt and tore at the stout paper packet sewn there. He ripped it out. The paper came forth red, and so did his hand. With fumbling fingers he rent aside the paper and opened the delicate little scarf of lace from the Ciudad Mexico. He dropped it over the poor twisted figure, then looked about. The horses were all gone. No matter. He would follow.

Sweat and bloody dust filled his eyes. He wiped them clear, expelled a deep breath, and strode away along the trail. He did not look back at the clearing. Now he had only one thought, remembered but one thing, one man.

AS HE came into the outer trail, he paused for a moment, stepped uncertainly, and put out his hand to a tree for support. Again he wiped his eyes, straightened up, and went on afresh, on out toward the hot sunlight beyond the trees.

Now it must be told of a man who was riding, alone, toward Gonzales with curious work to do there. A big man, carelessly dressed, with a bold, handsome face and very bright hot eyes. He came to an oak tree and saw a man sitting against it, leaning back against the tree, with eyes closed. He dismounted hastily and went to the man.

The Cibolero opened his eyes and looked up, dazedly.

"Here, what's happened?" demanded the stranger. "Looks like you been in a fight."

"Howdy," murmured the Cibolero. The stranger held a flask to his lips, aided him to swallow, then touched his ripped, stained buckskin shirt.

"Good God, man! You're all cut up!"

"Don't matter," said the Cibolero, heartened by the fiery drink. "One of 'em got away. I got to be after him—"

"What? Say, you don't mean a Mex soldier with his jaw 'most cut off? I found him laying dead in the road. Say, who in hell are you?"

The Cibolero suddenly smiled, and relaxed.

"A Texian, by God!" he said, and laughed faintly, although his eyes were blazing. "I tell you, one Texian is good for any ten of them yeller-bellies! Yeah; I'm a Texian, by God, from now on—on—"

His jaw fell, and his head lolled forward. The other man looked swiftly at his hurts, perceived that life was extinct, then straightened up.

"Texian, huh?" he murmured. "There's the answer to all these politicians. By godfrey, I'll be a Texian myself, and nothing else! Old Sam Houston's right. No more Americans, no more Mexican citizens—just Texians. Yes, sir, sure as my name's Jim Bowie, that's the answer! Shake, pardner. From now on, says you; and that goes double."

And leaning forward, Jim Bowie gravely shook the dead hand of the Cibolero.

II

THE SEVENTH CHILD

I WAS standing beside the wall of the ancient Conception Mission, outside San Antonio. Here had been the refectory of the monks, now destroyed on three sides, the walls pock-marked with bullet holes. It was here that James Bowie, most tragic of all the Texan heroes, had fought for freedom in 1835. And as I stood, an echo of voices came to me, then the words of a man singing. I was alone here, yet laughing tones sounded distinctly, until the lilting words reached to me more clearly.

"Yankees and courtly Spaniards, Tennessee mountaineers,
Creoles and Dutch and slavers (gentlemen in arrears)
Shoulder to shoulder gathered, answering blow with blow—
For by God, sir! We fought in Texas a hundred years ago!"

I listened, astonished. A raucous burst of cheering sounded from the air around. Then, amid thin drumming hoofbeats of spurring men, a ragged hearty chorus came to me, a chorus as of distant, shouting men:

"Here's to you, Colonel Bowie, damn your eyes!"

What did it mean? Not even a tourist was in sight; was this some delusion of the senses? And yet, men had died here for liberty a hundred years ago....

THE SALOON in San Felipe was well filled, and blue with tobacco smoke. Voices rose in a steady blare of sound. Here in San Felipe men were gathered from all over the Texas settlements in this year of 1835. A new government had been formed, but the convention was riddled with politics, jealousy and diversity of aims.

Alone at the end of the bar stood a man whose hat was pulled far over his eyes. He was drinking, and drinking hard. He had traveled hard to get here, he had spurred hard, day and night; and the man he had come to find was not here.

"Old Houston's plumb locoed!" rose a rough voice down the bar. "We got no call to fight Mexico. All we want is our own state gov'ment back again, ain't it?"

"And be a part of Mexico again? Not much!" shouted another man. "Houston's right. We got to cut loose and have our own republic. We can lick them greasers easy."

"And lose everything doing it, too. Fannin and Bowie and them crazy galoots are fighting along the Border now, raiding Mexican settlements and killing soldiers. Is it true that there's been a fight at Gonzales?"

"Dunno," came the reply. "Some rumors come in, that's all. If fighting's started, boys, hurray for it!"

Argument rose high and impassioned, as confused as the turmoil which prevailed all over Texas. And as it rose, an old Mexican woman came threading her way among the men, a crone whose black eyes glittered from beneath her black shawl. She spoke, now to one man, now to another; she was met with laughter or rebuffs.

The two men next the solitary drinker were engaged in hot argument. Both were from the Brazos settlements, big, powerful men, rough of tongue and of hand. One was discussing Jim Bowie in no uncertain terms.

"Calls hisself a colonel now, does he? Huh! Made his money running slaves. Married into a high-toned Spanish family in Bexar, got a big land grant, and now he's raiding the greasers on the Border. Santy Anny has put a price on his head. Drunken rat, that's what this Bowie is! Fighting grizzly, huh? Well, he's a hell of a man to be a Texian, and I don't care who hears me. Huh? Who in hell are you? I don't savvy your lingo."

The old crone was mumbling something. The other man laughed.

"She wants to tell your fortune, Joe."

"Fortune, hell! She's a spy, that's what." The first speaker flushed darkly, then reached out and gripped the crone by the shoulder. "Sneaking in here to listen. By God, if I had my way I'd hang every greaser in Texas. Come on, you, spit it out; who's paying you to spy on us, huh?"

The crone shrank back, the man gripping her the more fiercely.

The man at the end of the bar moved suddenly. He had hot bright eyes, very blue in color, with reddish brown side-whiskers. He came up to the three, and took hold of the man's wrist. His movements were surprisingly swift and agile.

"I reckon, suh, you aren't used to womanfolks," he said calmly. His words reached out upon the startled hush. "Apologize to the lady."

"Huh? Me apologize? Leggo my wrist, damn you!" cried out the big man. "Joe Harkness don't apologize to no Mexican slut—"

HIS VOICE died. The grip of the smaller man tightened on his wrist. His fingers loosened, and the old crone slipped away. A grimace of pain crossed his face, then he swung with his free hand. Instead of hitting the smaller man, he himself was hit across the mouth. He staggered back against the bar, and a knife flashed out in his hand.

"By God, you'll pay for that with your ears!" he roared out, passion flooding in his face. He was oblivious to the swift mutter going around the circle of watchers; he did not catch the name of "Jim Bowie!" that flashed from mouth to mouth. "I'll slit them ears off'n you for that, hear me!"

He hurled himself at the slim figure, but Bowie did not move or evade the rush. Instead, Bowie met him breast to breast, with

a ferocity that drew a gasp from those about. The two figures locked. Bowie caught the other's wrist in a steel grip—then suddenly lashed out with terrific speed and savagery.

The fight was over almost as it had started. Harkness staggered away and sank down, groaning. Bowie put away his pearl-handled knife.

"He won't die," he said calmly. "Better get a doctor, to make sure—"

"Jim Bowie!"

The words fairly exploded on the room from all sides, and men crowded in with delighted yells. Drinks were passed. Five

minutes later, the magnetic personality of the one man was dominating the whole place, for Jim Bowie had a peculiar charm that held men and gripped them.

They crowded about him in wonder and awe and friendship. Tales of him had gone afar. His prowess as a fighter was already a frontier fable, but he was also a great man, or had been. He had married into one of the proudest families of Mexico, he was wealthy, a golden future had opened out to him; then came the cholera and swept away his wife and children.

And now Jim Bowie was a heartbroken, terrible man who sought only liquor and freedom, for all life was wreckage behind him.

A gust of yells swept down the street. Men came running, bursting into the place.

"Hey! It's true, it's true!" arose the shout. "Fighting at Gonzales, and the boys there whipped the greasers! Licked the best cavalry a-going! Licked 'em!"

"Hear that, Bowie?" screamed somebody.

"I heard it a while back," he rejoined. "I just come from there."

The voices became frenzied, exultant; amid all the uproar, Jim Bowie slipped out unobserved. He passed around to the

side of the saloon and stood there in the darkness, trying to decide what to do. He had wanted to find Sam Houston, but Houston was away. As he stood, he could hear the wave upon wave of exultant shouting that spread through town. The finest cavalry of Mexico had been licked by a handful of Texians!

BOWIE GRIMACED sourly. He had been raiding the Mexicans down on the Border; he and Fannin had formed bands of hot-heads whose sole purpose was to clear Texas of the Mexican yoke. The deputies here in San Felipe did not know whether to fear or admire these raiders.

San Antonio, which the Texians called Bexar, was held by the Mexican General Cos with fifteen hundred men, and President Santa Anna was said to be moving north with a huge army. The half-organized settlers were in chaos. Houston was nominally in command of the army, but had no army. Politics seethed. Rivalries and jealousies were rife. There was no imminent crisis to spur either side to action, unless the battle at Gonzales should set a spark to the powder. Texas was in open revolt, but Cos hesitated to attack, and the settlers sparred for time. Patriotism was, as ever, the cloak of selfish interest.

Bowie heard a step beside him. A hand touched his arm; he recognized the old Mexican woman who had disappeared from the saloon.

"Señor, I owe you thanks, many thanks."

"It is nothing, señora. You had best stay away from such places." Bowie, who spoke her tongue fluently, pressed money into her palm. "Here, this may help you."

"May God requite you! Do you wish me to tell your destiny?"

"I have none." He perceived that he was quite unknown to her. "My destiny lies all in the past."

"There is always death," she said, with a cackle of stark mirth. "Are you curious?"

"No," grunted Bowie. "But if it will humor you, tell me when I shall die."

She took his hand, drew him over to the lighted window in front, and there peered attentively at his palm. Then she looked up into his bright blue eyes.

"Caballero, you are a seventh child."

Bowie started, then laughed. "True true!"

"The past—ah, what a life, what sorrows! *Qué lástima*—what a pity! But I shall tell you the truth, caballero. Death is not far away from you."

"So much the better." Bowie's voice was skeptical and harsh. "By a bullet?"

"No, caballero. I can see you very clearly, dying in bed—"

"In bed?" he broke in scornfully. "*Poder de dios!* Little you know me."

"You are a seventh child; I cannot mistake your future, caballero. You shall die in bed, with the arm of a woman about you—"

As though stung, Bowie jerked away his hand.

"You accursed liar! No woman has any place in my life—"

"By the mother of God, I speak the truth! You may believe me or not, but you shall die in bed—"

Bowie drew back, with a storm of objurgations in angry Spanish. "Devil, fly away with you and your croaking. It's impossible, absurd. Get out!"

HE THRUST her aside and went his way, anger spurring at his brain. The old fool was out of her head. A woman, indeed—die in bed! It was sheer lunacy. He, the most famed duelist and fighter on the frontier, die in bed! He, whose whole heart and soul had died with the woman and two children dead of cholera, have a woman's arms around him! It all angered him past bearing. Yet, how the devil had she known that he was a seventh child?

"Bowie! Hey, Jim, is that you?"

An indistinct figure was approaching him. Under the starlight, he could smell it before he could see it—an indescribable odor of sweat, liquor, horse. A man dusty like himself, whose seamed features suddenly came clear.

"Houston! Why, Sam, of all people! They told me you were out of town. I came here for a confab with you."

"Just got in." The two men struck hands heartily. "Heard you were here and come to run you down. I been ridin' for a week without takin' off my clothes. Come on to the shack; I got a room in back of a store, yonder. Need a drink powerful bad."

Houston's voice was weary, and his shoulders drooped. Like Bowie, he had the wreckage of life and greatness behind him; but, unlike Bowie, he aimed ever at a fresh career, a newer vision. A hard, rough, patient man, Houston's right arm was a bit stiff from an old shoulder wound that would never heal; his calm poise was fathomless.

The two walked along in silence. Presently they were ensconced in a littered room whose desk was heaped with documents and letters. Houston lit candles, then got out a whiskey jug and drank deeply. Bowie followed suit. With a sigh, Houston sank down on the tumbled blankets of the bed.

"Good to see you, Jim. I been orating all over, trying to raise men, and damned poor luck. Something's got to happen."

"I know it," said Bowie. "When are you folks going to settle on readjustment or liberty?"

"God knows. These damned politicians talk and talk. If I had some men, we'd take action durned quick. Jim, it's a mess," said Houston dejectedly. "They're all holding out to support the Mexican constitution of 1824. Damn it, they can't see the idea of liberty. They don't realize that we must have complete freedom or nothing!"

"Heard about the scrap at Gonzales?"

Houston nodded. "Austin's just gone there to take charge—"

"Then you'd better send somebody after him," Bowie said grimly. "I have three men camped outside town. One of 'em met me here tonight, just come from Bexar. He says General Cos is leaving in a few days with five hundred men for Gonzales to wipe it out."

Houston whistled softly. But Jim Bowie went on without pause.

"You know what that means. We got to carry the fight to him—drive him out of Bexar, drive every Mexican back across the Rio Grande! And I'm starting it. Fannin has thrown his men in with mine. We're riding for Goliad and we'll smash the garrison there, then turn and make for Bexar. Now, old hoss, say your piece!"

HOUSTON CAME to his feet and began to pace up and down. Fire gleamed in his eyes, his unshaven, grim features took on new life.

"Jim, that's great news! If Cos is attacking, then we can force things. I'll stay here, get the organization moving. Austin will whip up an army and move on Bexar—if you can answer for Goliad! That means everything."

"Upon my honor, Sam," said Bowie gravely. "The Mexicans will be chased out of Goliad if I have to do it by myself. But I shan't. Fannin's waiting for me. In three days, we'll have the town."

"I count on that, then," Houston said curtly. "But remember, Cos has artillery—"

"We have men, by God!" With a laugh, Bowie drank deeply. He knew that Bexar was the key to all Texas. "I'm sending word to Fannin that the army is on the move at last. I'll stop and scout Bexar a bit, and spread news there that the Texians are coming. That'll keep Cos from moving out—"

"Do it if you like, but it'll be known. We've a plague of spies here." Houston swung around, aflame with energy. "You've heard of Colonel Crockett? He's headed this way to throw in with us; I got a letter from him last week. I wish we could get hold of a few regular army officers, Jim! If we had Ben Milam and a few more like him—"

Bowie shook his head. Ben Milam had been a distinguished officer in both the American and Mexican armies. A representative in the Texas legislature at Coahuila, he had been flung into prison when Santa Anna dispersed the state government.

"Well, Sam, we haven't got him, that's all. By the way, how about making Fannin a colonel of volunteers? He's only a cap'n now, and if you folks would give him a rank he'd have more authority."

"Right. You also; I'll have it done tomorrow. What's that paper you've got?"

Bowie grinned and opened the printed broadside he had dug out of his pocket.

"Compliment. A proclamation ordering a bunch of Texians arrested on the charge of treason. Me and Travis and some more—"

"Why, damn you—hurray!" Houston seized the paper avidly, his eyes blazing. "Just the thing we need, Jim; glory be, now we'll stampede these fellows! I'll send the news on to Austin tonight. How long are you staying in town?"

"About two minutes more. Got to be moving. How soon do you reckon Austin can march?"

"At once, with this news you've brought to stir things up. Jim, you've turned darkness into glory! You can't imagine the jealousy, the squabbles, the petty politics, here! But now it's all different. We'll stampede 'em, and no mistake. I'll guarantee that Austin will march for Bexar inside of five days—if I can send him word that you're attacking Goliad."

"Send him word that Goliad has been captured," said Bowie soberly. "I mean it. You can gamble that much on me."

"Agreed." Houston seized his hand, looked into his eyes. "God bless you, Jim! Take care of yourself; you don't realize how much I'm counting on you in the days to come. We haven't many men like you."

"Damned good thing you haven't," said Bowie with a laugh, and crammed his hat over his eyes. Next moment, he was gone.

A S H E strode along the muddy road, heading for the edge of town where his companions were camped to await him, he became lost in bitter thought. He could not get that old crone out of mind.

Die in bed? Absurd. A woman's arms around him? The idea maddened him. That was the most unlikely of all fates for Jim Bowie—partner of Lafitte the pirate, slave-runner, grandee and landowner, mill-owner, son-in-law of the great Veramendi, and now a broken man and hopeless. It was true, however, that he had been the seventh child. How the devil did that old hag guess it? Or did she have second sight?

His morose meditations were abruptly shattered. Too late, he wakened to dim shadows closing in upon him. A terrific blow on the back of the head crushed his hat and sent him staggering, to fall upon his face in a daze. Only the stout beaver hat saved him from complete oblivion.

He lay motionless, half-stunned, and to all appearance dead.

"Excellent work, my Diego!" sounded a Mexican voice. "It was the blow of a true caballero. We are sure of our money now; dead or alive, said the general. Ha, Mendez! Go you and fetch the other men and the horses, while we tie him hard and fast. Dead or not, he is a devil incarnate and safer if well tied. Hurry!"

There was a soft pad-pad of moccasined feet receding into the obscurity.

"Where is the riata, Diego?" came the voice again. Bowie's head was clearing. His thoughts went swiftly back to that night in Natches-under-the-Hill when, prone upon a saloon floor, he had knifed two men to death. Hard-fighting men. He smiled grimly as he lay.

"Alive or dead, once he reaches San Antonio, the money is ours. You have a good eye, my Diego; you did well to recognize him in that saloon. And it was a lovely blow. Well, take him by the feet; I'll tie up his arms. Wind the riata into the flesh, mind; we must take no chances, for this Bui is a devil. Here, turn him over."

Bowie's figure was rolled over in the mud. Hands seized upon his left arm, but the fingers of his right hand had already closed on the pearl haft of his knife.

The knife drove suddenly upward. There was a choked cry, then a furious and deadly struggle took place in the darkness. One man fell forward, his weight lying across the legs of Bowie and pinning him down as the second Mexican drove in with knife stabbing viciously.

Somehow, Bowie avoided that frantic, panicky stroke. His left hand caught the assailant and dragged him down, with remorseless grip. What passed in the obscurity was impossible to say. Presently there was a bleating cry, then a slapping of spasmodic feet against the ground, and silence.

THE HARSH, mirthless laugh of Jim Bowie sounded. He rose, picked up his crushed hat, and went staggering away. His head was still ringing from that blow; but, if a blow is to change the current of history, there must be no error in its delivery.

Now across the autumn plains of Texas, men spurred fast. Vigilance committees were formed, from near and far the summons brought men with their rifles and powder-horns to gather at Gonzales and elsewhere. Rumors were startling— some said that Goliad had been taken, others said that General Cos was marching on San Felipe. Couriers killed their horses, dust-white men rode shouting past groups of cabins, and from Louisiana parties of frontiersmen were heading fast and hard for Texas. What was actually happening, what would soon happen, no one dared to say.

Upon a chill evening, with a serape flung about his shoulders, Jim Bowie swaggered past the sentinels at the ford, and made his way into Bexar. His glib Spanish tongue, his forged papers, gained him free passage from the ex-convicts in Mexican uniform.

Old Bexar was purely a Mexican city, save for a few American traders. As he strolled about, Bowie was chuckling to himself at the changes in the town he knew so well. Far from marching against the settlers at Gonzales, shrewd General Cos had flung all his energy into preparing against the Texian attack. The stone houses were converted into forts, the streets were barricaded and commanded by batteries of artillery.

Across the river lay the old San Antonio mission, now called the Alamo because a company of soldiers from Alamo de Parras, in old Mexico, had once garrisoned it. It was vastly altered; the outer arches were gone, pulled down to help make a rubble heap, over which artillery could be pulled to the roofs. The barracks windows had been walled up, entrenchments and batteries and outer works had been constructed,, and there was not such another fortress in all Texas. No Texian army, without artillery, could take this place.

Bowie was inclined to agree with his Mexican assurance. He turned back into the town and presently came to a halt on the bridge across the upper stream. He stood in moody abstraction, his figure dimly revealed by the starlight, listening to the idle talk of soldiers and women strolling by the stream. Death to the Texian traitors; no quarter; the plunder and loot of land and settlements—he vaguely heard the words, but paid scant attention.

For, there close by, were the lights of the one place he might still call home: the Veramendi mansion with its pleasant gardens. There, as elsewhere, he was welcome. All about in this city were warm sympathizers with the cause of Texas; here were friends, relatives, helpers. Yet he stood alone, staring grimly at the place.

ALONE; HE would always be alone now. In that house he had lived and loved and won. Ursula Veramendi, fairest of all Texian women, was his bride. From here he had taken her to Saltillo and built his cotton mills; glittering vistas of wealth, position, influence were open to him. The two children whom he idolized had been born here in this house, had been baptized in the church across the plaza. And then the swift coming of cholera, and everything swept away in a day. Everything except the wealth which he cursed and flung aside.

He pulled his serape closer, staring moodily at the house where he would be so warmly welcomed, did he but make himself known. So he would die in a bed, eh? His harsh laugh sounded softly. He, who had not so much as a bed to his name! Yet the old hag had sworn by the Virgin that she told the truth. Bah! He shrugged and turned away. He was alone, yes, but there remained Texas. Here was something to work for, to fight for, to give himself for; a cause, the only thing left in life. A thing intangible, without self-interest....

"Señor Bui!"

At the soft voice, Bowie turned quickly; his name was pronounced alike in Spanish or English. Close to him in the darkness stood a Mexican soldier, uniform untidy in the starlight, *cigarillo* gleaming with a red point, hat pulled low.

"You speak to me, caballero?" Bowie said quietly, hand on knife.

"But yes," was the response. "I recognize you, señor. You are, no doubt, spying upon our glorious city, upon our *soldados,* our dispositions—"

Bowie's left arm shot out. He caught the speaker by the tunic and was in the very act of stabbing when he was paralyzed in every nerve.

"Hey! For gosh sake, Jim, hold on! It's me, 'Rastus Smith!"

"Deaf Smith!" Bowie drew a deep breath. Another instant, and he would have killed the most famous scout and spy on the frontier. The two of them stood quite alone.

"Why, you damned fool, trying out your jokes on me! You ought to have a knife in your gizzard; and you came close to it. Where'd you get that uniform?"

"Took it off a greaser; he didn't need it no more. By gosh, you've got a grip! I been follerin' you quite a spell. Thinks I, that ain't Jim Bowie, but it sure is Jim's walk. I'm on my way to locate you at Goliad."

"You look it," snapped Bowie, throwing an affectionate arm about the shoulders of the taller man. "How'd you know I was here?"

"Didn't. Just took a notion to scout Bexar a bit, and seen you. I hear they got Maverick and the other Americans here safe in jail."

"And cannon to hold the place. Anybody send you to find me?"

"Yeah," said Deaf Smith. "Gin'ral Austin allowed I might locate you. Seems like the boys are all het up over Goliad being captured."

Bowie laughed softly. "It will be, day after tomorrow. What's your message?"

"Well, Austin's getting the army on the move. Marching tomorrow."

"Marching?"

"Sure. Heading for Bexar lickety-split; coming like hell, Jim. Austin says for you and Fannin to fetch along your outfits and scout the place, and get a good spot for a camp. He's durned uneasy and wants to be sure you're ready to join up."

"Take back word that we're ready and waiting," said Bowie, a warm vibrancy in his words. "I got to meet Fannin and jump those Mexicans in Goliad."

Deaf Smith chuckled. "You don't need to hurry, Jim."

"Eh?" Bowie stared at him in the starlight. "What do you mean?"

"You'll be too late, I reckon. I met up with a feller on my way here, one of them settlers under Cap'n Collingsworth."

"Yes; he was going to raise men and meet us at Goliad."

"I reckon he's done took Goliad already, Jim. This feller allows that Collingsworth got tired of waiting for you and Fannin to come along and was a-heading for Goliad hisself. Aimed to git there yesterday and jump the place. He had forty-odd men."

Bowie whistled. "And Colonel Sandoval there has a hundred Mexicans with cannon—good lord! I've got to be off—"

They moved off, and the obscurity swallowed them up.

IN DEFIANCE of the rainy season, Austin's alleged army was moving forward on Bexar. Sam Houston had sent out a call for five thousand men; five hundred responded. An army without artillery, with little powder, with no discipline. From New Orleans came the Grays, a troop of adventurers burning to liberate Texas, only to find that Texas had no anxiety to be liberated, but wanted to stay in the Mexican federation.

Desperately, vainly, Steve Austin endeavored to beat some cohesion into his rabble. These settlers, hunters, adventurers would acknowledge no authority, and jeered at orders which did not suit them. At the moment, they were aflame with zealous ardor, but not to the point of facing the artillery of General Cos.

Great news reached them. Collingsworth had taken Goliad by assault. Colonel Ben Milam had unexpectedly appeared, having escaped from his Mexican prison. Bowie and Fannin were scouring the plains. With wild cheers, the army pressed on to Salado, five miles from Bexar, and settled in camp. Here Bowie joined them, with Fannin, Milam and ninety men, to be received with great acclaim.

Privately, however, Austin was hopeless and despondent.

"What can we do against Mexican discipline and cannon?" he said to Bowie that night. "And we're far outnumbered."

"What of it? What are you here for?" Bowie snapped.

"To hold Cos in check and gain time. More men are on the march. We have a cannon and ammunition coming sometime. We can't assault Bexar, of course; we'll form a secure camp outside town and wait for reinforcements. Have you selected any camp site?"

"Hell, no. One of the missions might do."

"Then suppose you go ahead tomorrow with your company, choose a secure spot, and we'll move up. Cheer up, Jim; in a week's time we'll have a thousand men gathered!"

Bowie, disgusted, yet realizing the hard sense of Austin's viewpoint, acceded. There was but one gleam of light. Mexican prisoners reported that General Cos, astounded by the assault and capture of Goliad, intended to stay safe behind his defenses.

With morning, Bowie and Fannin moved their ninety men ahead. Bowie had already decided that the Concepcion Mission presented the desired site, as it was on the river and close to Bexar.

EVENING FOUND him camped in and around the outlying mission buildings. He was in morose, surly humor. The prospect of capturing Bexar seemed fantastic, for the boasted army of Texas was no more than a straggling mob of riflemen.

With daybreak, he rose feeling feverish and uncertain. Outside, the camp was rolled in a blanket of dense fog, so thick that nothing could be seen fifty feet away. Bowie went to one of the outposts, and stood talking with the men there. After a little, he knelt and put an ear to the ground.

"Strange!" he said, "I could have sworn that I heard voices and hoof beats. You've seen nothing all night?"

"Nary a thing, Cunnel," was the response. "All quiet."

Rejoining Fannin for breakfast, Bowie had barely risen from table when a man came running and shouting that he had seen Mexican lancers in the trees, at the south end of camp. While a laugh went up at his expense, there came a yell from the northern outpost, then a discharge of pistols. Instantly, the camp leaped into activity.

"Looks like they're all around us, Jim," said Fannin coolly. "Who'd have thought old Cos would have the nerve to attack!"

Bowie grunted. Before he could reply, the fog was split by a blazing volley of musketry, and as bullets rained upon the camp, the shrill voices of Mexican bugles began to blare unseen.

Volley after volley was poured into the camp from all directions. That they were completely surrounded was now obvious to all; but the men were kept out of sight, and ordered to shelter among the trees and vines below the mission buildings. Until the fog lifted, nothing could be done.

The sun rose, and gradually the fog began to clear. The Mexican fire had ceased; Bowie waited, impatient and anxious. That his force was surrounded and cut off, he quite realized. His head ached, and he knew now that fever had seized upon him.

A shout pealed up, and another. "There they are!"

To the right of the camp, the thinning fog disclosed lines of infantry deploying. Cavalry were wheeling and taking position. A cannon was being brought up and placed in readiness. Fannin uttered a cool laugh.

"Looks like they're out to get us, Jim! How many do you make it?"

"Four hundred, about," Bowie rejoined.

"Thought so. Orders?"

"Take the south side. I'll take the north—"

A rifle cracked. The battle had begun.

Bowie kept his men under cover, restrained their fire, and waited. From the Mexican lines, volley after volley rang out in an almost continuous fire that did little damage, except to the mission buildings. Estimating that the cannon was not more than eighty yards distant, Bowie, picking out his best riflemen, sent them forward to open fire upon it.

"Spread out, boys, and let 'em have it!"

As he spoke, the cannon erupted in smoke. A storm of grape and cannister whined through the brush. Immediately after, the bugles shrilled, and the lines of cavalry wheeled into a charge.

A RIPPLE of rifle-fire broke out from the Texian lines. The men serving the cannon were dropped as though by magic. The cavalry fell into confusion; men and horses rolled in the brush, the charge was broken. A ragged cheer rang out, to be instantly checked as the lines reformed. The artillerymen, although dropping fast under the galling fire, served their piece bravely. Again it spouted death, and again.

The cavalry, spreading out now, came galloping and thundering forward, carbines banging, pennons and lances glittering. Again their ranks fell into disorder, as death smote among them. The gold-laced officers suffered heavily. Bowie, yelling with sheer frenzied delight, saw the charge broken and falling back.

"We've got 'em, boys, we've got 'em!" he shouted. "Get on up closer around that cannon! If they try it again, go for 'em!"

The cannon crashed out. The man next to Bowie coughed and fell against him with a spurt of lifeblood; grape shrieked through the air.

The infantry lines were wavering; most of their officers were down by this time. Their blaze of fire continued, but the bullets went high. Now the bugles were again shrilling, the squadrons of horsemen reformed. From the ground between, where horses kicked and men lay heaped, arose a terrible sound of shrieks and groans, drowned out by the crack of rifles.

The men around the cannon fell fast, yet it was fired again, and yet again, holding the Texian riflemen in check. The cavalry spread out farther, ringing in the whole position, the bugles sounded the charge. This time they meant business.

They swept forward with shrill yells. The rifles began their deadly cracking, front rank firing then falling back to reload while the second rank fired. Officers went down. The ranks were broken, went sweeping aside in wild disorder.

"Go get 'em!" yelled Bowie, and his men obeyed.

Forth from their covert for the first time broke the Texians. They charged upon the cannon, they went running at the infantry lines, hurled themselves at the broken cavalry. A panicky bugler sounded the retreat.

The lines broke and fled. The cannon was abandoned. The lancers and dragoons headed about in precipitate flight for Bexar's protection. The ninety had smashed the four hundred, captured their positions and their cannon.

Fannin and Bowie slapped each other on the back, dancing about in boyish exultation. Men shouted until they were hoarse, ran down horses and captured them, brought in the wounded, looted the dead.

"Jim, after this we can do anything!" exclaimed Fannin eagerly. "If we had the army here, we could keep 'em on the run and take Bexar!"

"Sure, but there's no army," said Bowie drily. His face was hot and flushed, his eyes very bright. Fannin surveyed him with a frown.

"Looks to me like you got fever, Jim."

"I know it. No matter. Come on, we got plenty to do!"

Plenty to do, yes—couriers to send out, wounded to take care of, dead to bury. Bowie settled down to write his report. The words came hard.

"I reckon I need a drink," he murmured, and got it. Then he

looked down at a ragged wound in his coat—a bullet had torn through, not touching him. He broke into his harsh, mirthless laugh.

"I always heard a seventh child was born lucky," he observed. "Reckon it's so, too. And maybe that old hag knew her business. By godfrey, I may have to die in bed yet, just to prove that she did! I'm sure going to be ill. And if I am—"

His eyes warmed suddenly. Old Ben Milam, of course! There was the man to take over the company from him, if he was ill. Ben Milam!

III

THE JAILBIRD

UPON a gray December dawn, I crossed one of the river-bridges in San Antonio and came to a halt beside an ugly modern storefront. Here had stood the old Veramendi mansion with its gardens— gone now. The street lights glimmered fitfully. A thread of mist rose from the river.

Somewhere a voice lifted. Some homeward-bound drunk, I thought; but no! It was a gay voice, ringing and vibrant and clear, a voice to stir the blood. The words actually echoed from the storefront nearby, and reached me, distinctly. The lilt of song came clear:

"We didn't have much book-learning, we knew the feel of dirt,
  Some of us had fine manners, and some of us lacked a shirt;
  We could shoot or swing a broadaxe, handle a pick or hoe—
  And by God, sir! We fought for Texas, a hundred years ago!"

Thin and far, a burst of raucous laughter and wild cheering seemed to float from the moonstruck clouds overhead. Voices broke forth in unison:

"Here's to you, Old Ben Milam, damn your eyes!"

No one. Nothing in sight; the street was empty. Imagination? Yet on this very spot, a hundred years ago almost to a day, a man had died. That old Veramendi mansion had witnessed strange scenes, a corpse laid to rest at low twelve with Masonic ritual while bullets shrieked around....

TWO MEN paused at the entry to a trench running across the street, running across to the Veramendi gardens.

Rifles were cracking, musketry was ringing out in continuous uproar, cannon were smashing away at every moment. Down the street, over the barricade of the trench, bullets were hailing. Dirt was flying. Discharges of grape went screaming in ricochet from the stones, threw earth and splinters everywhere.

"Down, Ben! Down!" exclaimed one of the two men. "Stoop as you go across!"

"Be damned if I will," and the other man laughed gaily—a

deep, vibrant laugh. "I'll stoop for no Mexican! Those fellows can't shoot, anyhow. Come on!"

He started across. What thoughts were in his mind, what retrospect of life past, of glorious adventure, came to Old Ben Milam in this moment? He was barely forty-five as he strode along, head high, a gay smile on his lips.

HIS THOUGHTS went back to Monterey. There, the previous fall, he broke jail. Alone, empty-handed with a stolen horse, he set out to cross seven hundred miles of savage trackless desert. He was being hunted near and far.

Weeks later, starving, haggard, worn to the bone, he prowled about the wretched collection of adobe huts by the Rio Grande which was named Laredo. He was waiting his chance to steal a chicken or anything else eatable, and get along. Voices reached him as he crouched in the brush.

"Keep an eye out, Manuel. The others are to keep a sharp watch for that mad Americano who escaped from Monterey. El Coronel Milam."

"Colonel Milam?" echoed another voice in surprise. "But I know him well. He is no Americano; he is of Mexico, señor! I have served in his regiment. He is one of the legislature from the state of Texas—"

"No matter. He's a rebel, to be shot on sight."

Milam grinned to himself as he listened.

ALL HIS life had been a record of wild adventure. In the War of 1812 he distinguished himself. A Kentuckian of little education, he had something better—ability to win men's affection, to make them follow him.

He plunged into filibustering, joined Lafitte the pirate, came to Mexico as an adventurer. Since then he had been, as they said, in every Mexican jail. He helped Mexico win independence. When Iturbide seized power as emperor, Milam held out for freedom—and went to prison. He escaped, went on fighting; was given a million acres of land and became affluent. He went down to Coahuila as a member of the legislature from Texas.

Then Santa Anna struck, overthrowing the Mexican constitution and proclaiming himself dictator. Ben Milam, like other Americans caught in the net, went into jail; but jails did not hold him long. He got out, got a horse—and here he was.

Such was the man who crouched there, biding his time.

Presently the time came. He darted in upon the empty hut, made away with a little corn and a fowl, and with darkness to aid him, regained his skeleton horse. That night he swam the Rio Grande.

More desert ahead, empty Texan plains, and he had to keep far from roads, pushing on by star and sun, living on berries and nuts and grass and cactus-pears. No safety for him until he reached the American settlements to the north of Bexar.

Weeks later, his horse a staggering ruin, he himself was at the last gasp and worn to a shadow. His clothes were rags. Shaggy beard and hair uncut, he looked like nothing human. And then, one afternoon, he looked down the blinding sunset lane of light, and saw three horsemen making for him. He was caught.

Ben Milam had no intention of going back to jail, however. Desperate, he sent its poor beast toward a clump of trees, gained the cover, and slid to earth. Where he was, he had not the least idea. A good hundred miles from safety, at least; he had covered six hundred or so, by his figures. He whipped out his knife, got his back against a tree, and blinked at the three riders who came spurring in at him.

"Hey, Bill!" broke out one of the three, in astonishment at close view of this gaunt scarecrow. "He don't look like no Mexican!"

A gasp broke from Milam. Then a cry.

"Hey! Are you fellers Americans?"

"You're durned right we are," came the response. "Took you to be a Mexican. Who are you?"

Milam dropped his knife and reeled forward.

"Ben Milam. For God's sake give me a bite to eat—"

MILAM! WITH whoops of joy, the three surrounded him. They shared their clothes with him, plied him with food and water. Suddenly, at their words, he jerked up his head and stared.

"What's that? Looking for Mexicans? What d'you mean?"

"Ain't many left loose," and one man grinned. "Didn't you hear about the fight up to Gonzales?"

"Fight?" Ben Milam's eyes flashed. "Good Lord! You don't mean Texas is fighting? And me in jail down there! Is it true?"

"You bet. We got forty-odd men down the river with Cap Collingsworth. We're aiming to jump Goliad tonight. Jim Bowie's got another crowd a-coming but we sort o' lost ourselves."

"Hurray! Count me in!" cried Milam eagerly. "All I want is to get a good whack at those Mexicans! And you've actually had fighting?"

"Sure thing. We've done kicked the Mexicans out of Anahuac and all the other places down to the Gulf, except Goliad and

Bexar. And there's an army coming to kick 'em out o' Bexar likewise. We got one hell of an army, lemme tell you—"

Texas was up and fighting, then! On the moment, Ben Milam was like a new man, alive with fire and energy. None the less, that horrible march north had grayed his hair and beard. He was Old Man Milam now, to everyone.

But he was safe at last; and that night, in the camp down the river, his arrival electrified Captain Collingsworth's little band of settlers. He had been given up for dead; but now the name of Milam was a thing to conjure with. His gay, eager spirit, his fiery energy, had made him one of the most popular men in Texas.

Despite his military training, his rank in the Mexican army, he refused bluntly to be elected as an officer. He insisted on joining up as a volunteer private. Texas in revolt! The dream of his life had come true.

The gray light of dawn; and before them lay the town of Goliad, with its stores, its arms, its ammunition. Here was the only fortified place in Texas, outside Bexar itself, with a hundred men in garrison.

The forty-eight men crept forward in the obscurity. A sentinel challenged them, yelled in alarm, fired. Rifle-bullets cut him down. Men armed with axes smashed at the gates. The quarters of the commandant were stormed.

In ten minutes Goliad was taken, its garrison were prisoners or fugitives, and Old Ben Milam had struck his first blow for Texas.

N O W F R O M east and north a storm of men concentrated upon San Antonio, then known to one and all as Bexar. The so-called army of Texas marched from Gonzales; men came from the Border villages, from the Gulf coast, outlaws and men proscribed. Adventurers from Mississippi and Louisiana, in full company and gay uniform. They came gaily on, convinced that one Texian could put to flight a hundred Mexicans, cocksure in the belief that General Cos would surrender abjectly at the first summons. They recked nothing of his fifteen hundred regulars, his score of cannon and his ample fortifications.

All of them knew Ben Milam or had heard of him. He attached himself to Jim Bowie and the impetuous Fannin—hard-fighting, hard-living Jim Bowie, who had a force of guerrilla riders. They came pouring down to Bexar, men without discipline, order or artillery, burning to be at Mexican throats, fighting among themselves—eager to fight for the status of Texas as part of the Mexican federation. Few of them talked of liberty, of cutting the state from the union. They knew not whom they obeyed, were careless of authority, laughed at orders.

Suddenly came the fight at Concepcion Mission, outside the town, when Bowie and Fannin, with ninety men, whipped the four hundred. There came the "grass fight," when Mexican foraging parties were driven madly in upon their fortifications by Bowie and Ben Milam. These encounters gave the enemy abrupt pause.

These Americanos were not men, but devils. To fight them openly were utter folly. And the fortifications, the artillery, the unexpected odds against them, gave most of the Texians even more abrupt pause.

Who held Bexar, held Texas—and General Cos meant to hold Bexar. He said as much, with his calm, disdainful smile, when he was summoned to hand over the town. Mexico would not treat with rebels, except at the point of the bayonet. There was a price on the head of their leaders; let them disperse! All American traders inside Bexar were clapped into jail. Over the Alamo was hoisted the scarlet flag—no quarter to rebels!

Rebels? Jim Bowie, Milam and a third of the army hooted at the word. The other two-thirds, including the leaders, thought twice. Actual rebellion meant loss of lands, position, estate. Many in the army were Mexicans who had joined the Texan cause, but not to cut loose from Mexico. Indecision arose, for here faint hearts held the reins. Steve Austin departed to raise more men and money, and General Burleson took over the army.

Deaf Smith, the scout, got news in plenty out of the town, and no happy news, either. Even Ben Milam, who was all for a headlong smash, paused and blinked when he heard about it.

H A L F A mile outside town, the army encamped and pondered sadly. Weeks passed, nothing was done; General Burleson took command, and he was a cautious gentleman. Old Ben Milam raged and ranted and drank, and nothing was done. General Cos was afraid to come out, and Burleson was afraid to go in—and well he might be. The settlers began to drift away, back to their farms and families. Food and ammunition were low. Within the ranks, dissension, quarrels, sectional differences, arose.

Most of the army wanted nothing more than to keep Texas in the Mexican federation. A few wild, bold spirits, like Sam Houston, Bowie, and Ben Milam, were for independence.

And there lay Bexar, with General Cos laughing up his sleeve and waiting for them to come into his trap. A strong trap. The houses were nearly all of solid stone, and had been converted into loopholed forts. The streets were entrenched and barricaded.

Artillery commanded every approach. The old mission outside town, known as the Alamo, had been converted into a stout fort, armed with cannon on roof and wall, with outer breastworks and batteries ready. Every street, every entry, each of the two plazas, could be swept with bullets. To attack, without artillery preparation, would be slaughter.

So said General Burleson. So said all cautious spirits. Colonel Ben Milam fumed, and plenty of others with him. Ill feeling grew and became violent. November had passed. The bleak winter season was at hand, and nothing done, nothing attempted. Came the fourth of December.

Old Ben Milam and a riotous, unruly throng were gathered in the officers' quarters. A Mexican deserter had come in with word that there was disaffection among the Mexican troops, that the defenses were not so strong after all. As Milam and the others once again canvassed the situation, the bombshell broke. One of the New Orleans Grays came running in.

"All over, boys!" he panted. "Orders just been given out from headquarters. We're marching tonight."

"What?" yelled Milam in delight. "Attack?"

"Hell, no," was the disgusted response. "March begins at seven o'clock. The siege is done with. We're going into winter quarters down by Goliad."

There was one blank moment of incredulity. Then followed a storm of oaths. Milam was the first man outside and heading on a run for Burleson's headquarters.

True? The news was only too true. The orders were posted. The Texan "army" was to march away at seven that night.

"Like hell it will!" said Milam, white with shame and rage. "I came here to fight, not to sit on my heels all winter. By the Eternal, I'm going into Bexar if no body else goes!" He lifted his voice. Like a bugle-note, that blaring shout of his lifted over the tumult and quelled it, with words that were to ring down in history.

"Who'll go into Bexar with Old Ben Milam?"

THERE WAS a frenzied chorus of yells. A Border hunter yelled out something about "bear" and "Bexar"—both words being alike on American tongues. Word was flashed through the camp. More men came on the run. The crowd grew by leaps and bounds, literally.

"Old Ben Milam's going into Bexar, boys! Come on!"

General Burleson appeared, furious. He attempted to quell the tumult, to enforce discipline, commanding Milam and the others to disperse and give up their mad purpose. He was hooted down, jeered down; discipline, so far as he was concerned, was at an end.

Of the eight hundred men in camp there, three hundred and one threw in their lot with insanity. On the spot, Milam was elected to command the attack. He ordered the volunteers to disperse, and meet him at seven that night by the old mill on the river.

There, with torches flaring, Milam gave his orders. The three hundred were to attack at dawn—he himself by Acequia Street, Colonel Johnson with the second column by Soledad Street, the two avenues leading into the heart of the town. A deputation waited on the general, requesting him to postpone his runaway march until the result of the insanity was known; which, as one chronicler says, Burleson "very cheerfully" agreed to do. He even agreed to send some of his five hundred regulars to make a feigned attack on the Alamo, on the other side of town, while Milam attacked. And this was all he did do.

Daylight approached. The feigned attack on the Alamo began, completely holding the attention of the garrison—and as soon as Milam's rifles were heard, the "regulars" calmly marched back to Burleson's camp, leaving Milam to his fate.

These two streets were completely commanded by fortifications and batteries. Milam, with Deaf Smith scouting in the van, led his column straight ahead. A sentry fired, and Deaf Smith's bullet killed him. Five minutes later, Johnson's column was in control of the Veramendi mansion and gardens, while Milam and his men occupied the De la Garza house. These two houses were opposite each other, but there was no communication between them; each of the two converging streets entered the main plaza a hundred yards away. That hundred yards was composed of fortified houses, breastworks, batteries.

A tremendous fire was opened upon the two positions. All day long, grape and musketry poured forth, while Milam and Johnson consolidated their gains and dug in. With night, they fell to work opening a trench communication between the two houses, and by dawn, accomplished this. Throughout the night, the cannon never ceased to thunder.

Morning of the 6th found Milam's force in desperate position. Despite the trench, communication was risky, for it was under constant fire. Mexican sharpshooters had spread out on all sides, along the river and on housetops, and the cannon of the Alamo maintained a galling fire of grape. Milam's men, however, had brought up a small cannon, and opened a return fire with this. His riflemen began to work out, and pick off the enemy.

"Nothing for it but to go ahead," said he. "Let's go!"

WITH THE 7th, Milam was more stubborn than ever. One house, surrounded by an open space, lay between him and the buildings on the plaza. He ordered every man out with a rifle, and this tremendous and deadly fire swept the Mexican trenches clear, silenced the batteries temporarily, and cleared the sharpshooters from the housetops. In the lull, one Henry Karnes, an enthusiastic adherent of Old Ben Milam, grabbed a crowbar and ran for the house across the open. Muskets rained bullets, but he made the house in safety, and by the time a flood of men had followed him, smashed a way in. The house was captured. Milam was almost to the plaza now—but Johnson was still blocked from any advance.

Maverick, a trader who took an active part in the assault, attempted that afternoon to map out some course of action with Ben Milam. They inspected the newly captured house, which drove like a wedge at the buildings around the plaza.

"Can't get there by the streets," said Milam, as a hurtling storm of grape whistled overhead from the battery fifty yards away. "But we might smash into one of those houses and get a footing on the plaza itself."

"The men are staggering on their feet, Ben," said Maverick. "So are we. No sleep, mighty little grub, no rest. The church roof, the house roofs, are crowded with men ready to open fire on any advance. And their artillery—whew! Listen to it!"

As afternoon waned, indeed, the cannon from the Alamo had gradually opened up a regular and sustained fire, so well-directed that any communication, even by the trench, was hazardous in the extreme. Milam cursed the squatting camp outside town.

"Five hundred fresh men out there, and nary a one of them lending a hand!" he said. "Well, I'll skip over to the Veramendi house, see Johnson, and arrange with him to make a joint attack at midnight."

"Don't do that," said Maverick in alarm. "Man, it'd be madness! At least, send word over. I'll take the message."

"Send anybody where I wouldn't go myself?" snorted Milam. "Not by a damned sight. I'm going over."

"Then I'll go along," the other rejoined. "Watch out, though. They've got sharpshooters in the trees along the river. Spreading out everywhere."

The two made their way back to where the communicating trenches began. At the gay smile, the hearty words of Milam, the weary, wounded, haggard men, resting and fighting by shifts, raised a feeble cheer. Milam conferred with his officers.

"We're going to rush 'em, boys," he said. "If we can drive 'em out of the Navarro house, we'll get into Zambrano Row through the walls—and we'll have a wedge driven in that'll split the log sure! Well, Sam, let's go."

THEY STEPPED down into the trench and made their way along. They came to the street, with the Veramendi house opposite. Musket-balls spattered the dirt, grape shrieked and whistled. Milam started across, laughing.

"Down, Ben, down!" cried Maverick. "Stoop as you go across—"

"Be damned if I will!" returned Milam. "I'll stoop for no Mexican. Those fellows can't shoot, anyhow. Come on—it's safe enough."

A group of men were waiting at the end of the trench. Milam waved his hand to them. Across the street now, and stepping out of the trench—

Milam staggered. Then he collapsed, and Sam Maverick caught him as he fell. The rifle-crack came from a cypress tree along the river.

He was shot through the brain.

They could not believe it for a moment. They looked down at him, stared one at another, as the dismayed word was passed along. Old Ben Milam—dead!

Darkness descended. The red flashes, the thunders of cannon, never ceased. Colonel Johnson called his officers and those of Milam together. Grim men, powder-smeared, unshaven, in no better case than the men they commanded. A brief colloquy, then Johnson was elected to the supreme command.

"All right, boys," he said. "Cannon or no cannon—let's go get that Navarro house right now. Make 'em pay for Ben Milam."

"Make 'em pay for Ben Milam!" The phrase flashed on, was caught up and repeated. Weariness was forgotten. If the Alamo flew the red flag of "no quarter"— then the Mexicans would get no quarter. "Make 'em pay for Ben Milam!"

They went rushing forth. They swooped down on the Navarro house, hammered a way in, fought from room to room. Even from the roof, the Mexicans resisted, firing down through holes cut—until they were cleared from here, also. The house was taken at last. Adjoining it was Zambrano Row, a long barrackslike series of rooms. Men fell savagely to work, attacking the walls between with pick and axe. A long job.

Midnight saw Ben Milam laid to rest, with balls whistling around, with grape hurtling through the trees; laid to rest while heads were bared in the darkness, lest lights give away the party, and while the words of the Masonic ritual were punctured by the blasts of cannon. And those who did not hold with Masonry, saluted Ben Milam in the fraternity of patriotism and a cause common to all. There were tears on bronzed haggard cheeks, and choked voices. Ben Milam was gone, but his memory would not be stilled.

The word went on. "Make 'em pay for Ben Milam, boys!"

Hour after hour. Rain damped the powder; the morning broke cold. Into the Navarro house came the Grays, fresh and vigorous. The breach went forward in the walls; at last they were through, pouring into Zambrano Row under a hail of bullets.

Through—and now it was hand to hand, savage, a struggle of ferocity on both sides, no quarter asked or given. Bowie knife met bayonet, rifle met musket. As each room was cleared, the thick partition walls had to be breached into the next.

IN THE midst of this, a ragged cheer went up. Exhausted, grimly fighting on with faces like corpses for want of sleep, men looked one at another. The ragged cheer echoed again. Laughter took it up, hysterical laughter. Reinforcements at last—a lieutenant and a few men from Burleson's camp. But others were coming. Shame had done its work at last. News of Ben Milam's death had put fire to the powder-train.

They came, indeed, with evening—men trooping along, fresh and eager, hurling themselves into the struggle, giving the exhausted volunteers a chance to drop and rest. But the Grays refused to yield the van to these late-comers. Zambrano Row was cleared now, and the wedge driven home that would split the log.

Before midnight, the Grays struck. A strong walled house that would command the main plaza, lay directly ahead; it was heavily occupied. The Grays struck it like a thunderbolt, breached the wall, poured in a withering fire, reached the house beyond and stormed it. Then they began to cut loopholes.

Cannon and musketry opened up. Hour after hour, until daylight, the Mexican batteries sent balls and grape smashing in. Daylight came, and the rifles began to answer back with deadly effect. The plaza was under their fire. Reinforcements streamed up; more rifles went into play. Johnson and his men were gathering for the assault on the houses beyond, when suddenly the cannon fire slackened, and halted. The din of musketry died out. There was a silence in the sunrise.

A white flag came into sight, borne by a number of officers coming from the Alamo. General Cos and his fifteen hundred had had enough.

Then, indeed, General Burleson and his staff marched into Bexar, captured by no fault or deed of his; and the spirit of Ben Milam must have roared with ironic laughter to hear the stately phrases of surrender dictated by the "regulars," while those who had followed Old Ben into Bexar licked their wounds and mourned their dead.

Five days later, all were gone. Cos and his Mexicans, dragoons and foot—a third of them chose to remain as Texians—marched out and away toward the Rio Grande. The last Mexican was gone from the soil of Texas. Burleson was gone, too, with his "regulars" and his staff. The army was gone, dispersed again to the settlements.

Colonel Johnson remained to hold the town he had won. And one other remained, deathless in death, the silver cord loosed and the golden bowl broken; he, the homeless, gone to his long home where he bides today under a slab of stone, a great rough ashlar like himself, that bears but the one word

MILAM

IV

THE RIFLEMAN

VERY late one night, I was standing by the bullet-scarred entrance to the old chapel of the Alamo, in darkness and silence. Around hummed and throbbed the citied life of San Antonio, ablaze with neon lights and loud with sound; but here was silence, where a hundred years ago Mexican soldiers had come charging to death. Upon this silence broke a voice, singing. Some radio, I thought. Yet the voice seemed to echo from the very stones beside me; presently the words came more clearly and distinctly—

"We gambled and chawed terbaccer, we did as we had a mind,

We'd fight for a horn of liquor, and we left our wives behind;

We scalped and we cussed and ranted, we could wrassle heel and toe—

And by God, sir! We wrassled for Texas a hundred years ago!"

Then there was a rush of voices together. This time from inside the dark closed chapel. I heard a trampling of feet, a storm of rough, hoarse accents in chorus:

"Here's to you, Davy Crockett, damn your eyes!"

Was it mere fancy? Impossible to say. Here had died men, rough, hearty, lusty men of a past century, who had wrangled, disobeyed orders, hesitated, and finally fought to the death. Very human men, no prating, smug heroes—

65

WASHINGTON'S BIRTHDAY had come with great celebration in San Antonio. The prolonged fandango had left headaches in its wake. On this morning after, really early afternoon, Colonel Davy Crockett of Tennessee was enjoying a horn of liquor in the back room of Colorado Smith's store.

Crockett was rough and hearty of speech and action. His shrewd gaze surveyed the red-headed Smith, and a quizzical expression lay in his bronzed, square-hewn features.

"Prime liquor, Red. Dog-gone, that sure was one wild night! I come to Texas looking for a scrap, and all I see is fandangoes. Pretty soon, me and Jim Bowie are going down into Mexico and lift some scalps, you bet. Say, is that there state convention up at San Felipe going to declare for independence or not?"

"Nobody knows what that bunch of politicians will do," said Smith disgustedly. "Sam Houston's the only real man in the whole crowd. He's for independence, but most of 'em want to

stay in Mexico as a state. Any news at the fort from Santa Anna's army?"

Crockett tasted the liquor, rolled it judicially on his tongue, and shook his head.

"Nope. Ain't no army, far's we can tell; looks like that's all hogwash. All hands wrangling and cussing at headquarters. Colonel Travis, he's got a new gray uniform and a commission, and allows he's the prime egg; and Jim Bowie allows he's in command. And both being Texas cunnels, and me only a Tennessee cunnel, I ain't claiming no command at all. The Mexicans have been chucked out o' Texas and now we got time to fight among ourselves. Well, suh, here's to your hopes!"

He drank solemnly, his twinkling eye belying his words. Smith, who was one of the two or three American merchants in Bexar—what is now San Antonio—followed suit. After the riotous celebration of last night they felt a drink necessary.

"I dunno, Davy," said Smith, reflectively. "There's plenty of Mexicans who are the salt o' the earth. There's plenty, like Captain Seguin, fighting with us Texians. But this here Santa Anna—well, he's plain bad. An opium fiend. When he does come, I'll gamble he raises hell."

Davy Crockett guffawed. "Say! I've heard that song and dance for months. When I got here, what happened? Ben Milam and three hundred men had kicked out Gin'ral Cos, his fifteen hundred, and all his cannon—booted his backside clear over the Border. I'm real disap'inted, Red. I ain't seen a scalp lifted yet."

"You will," said Smith ominously, and Crockett guffawed again.

Half a mile from town and across the river was the old Alamo chapel, fortified in case of need by Travis and his garrison of a hundred and fifty Texians. Like many another, Crockett had come as a volunteer to aid the cause of Texas—but at the moment this cause was in some doubt.

After sharp fighting, every Mexican soldier had been expelled from Texas. At San Felipe, a convention of settlers was now in session. Whether to secede from Mexico and declare Texas a republic, or come to terms with Santa Anna and remain as a state in the Mexican federation, was the burning issue. Santa Anna and his armies had started north long ago to crush the rebels of Texas, but where he was, nobody knew.

THE CONVENTION had named Sam Houston commander in chief of the Texian forces—but Houston had enemies. Few of the leaders would obey his orders, and the convention had deposed him again. Everything was in absolute chaos, in this February of 1836.

"I've heard that Houston ordered Colonel Travis to abandon Bexar," Smith said slowly. "You're a military man, Davy. What do you think of the situation?"

Crockett chuckled. "I'm like the feller put up a tree by a b'ar," he said. "My thoughts ain't suitable to utterance. We got a hundred and fifty men here in Bexar. Colonel Fannin is over to Goliad with three hundred men. Near as I can see, that's the whole dummed Texian army."

"Sure. But what about Houston's orders?"

"I reckon that's right. He tells Fannin to abandon Goliad

and fall back on the Guadalupe River—and Fannin thumbs his nose. He tells Travis to blow up the Alamo and abandon Bexar—and Travis thumbs his nose. Them boys ain't running from no yeller belly Mexican general, and allows as much. And now who's in command? Nobody knows, and every feller is baiting a hook to catch the fish."

"Well, I don't like it," said Smith anxiously. "We drove out the Mexicans last year—"

"And that's just the trouble," broke in Crockett shrewdly. "You-all drove 'em out and allowed Mexico was licked. Then the dummed politicians got busy, and instead of being a republic like Sam Houston wanted from the first, what is it? Look at the flag acrost the river. We're fighting for Mexico, durn it!"

True. Over the Alamo floated the striped flag of republican Mexico with the date of 1824, when its constitution was adopted. Santa Anna, proclaiming himself dictator, had abolished that constitution. Texas alone resisted his dictatorship; and now, in its lack of all discipline and cohesion, Texas was about to suffer his wrath. Goliad and the Alamo were the only points which could pretend to fortification.

Shrill voices suddenly rang out from the street and the store front. Smith went to see what was up. Colonel Crockett, who understood no Spanish, leisurely poured himself another drink; when it came to hunting or drinking, speechifying or fighting, he was ever in the forefront.

SUDDENLY SMITH came rushing into the back room, blazing with excitement.

"Good God! The Mexicans are here, Davy—the dragoons are coming from San Pedro Hill this minute! Santa Anna's almost in the town itself. Run for it, man! We're caught!"

As though to emphasize his wild cry, the heavy report of an alarm-cannon boomed forth, and a tumult of voices eddied up after it.

By the time they reached the street the whole town was in uproar and confusion. The Mexican dragoons were, indeed, among the outlying farms. Due to the rival factions of Bowie and Travis, the garrison had sent out no scouts, and was totally unaware of Santa Anna's rapid advance. The surprise was complete.

The town itself was defenseless, with so small a body of garrison. The Alamo was the one rallying point. Crockett found himself running with the rest, through the streets to the river and across to the fortress. Mexicans, women, Americans—all poured in wild panic past him. Shopkeepers abandoned their stores and ran for it. Captain Dickinson, with his wife and child, dashed along on horseback, better late than never.

No quarter! Santa Anna had sworn it, and the thought was in all minds.

The buildings of the Alamo were ample. About the little chapel centered breastworks, batteries, enclosures for cattle; to the right stretched two-story barracks, with batteries defending them. The whole covered about two acres.

Once he reached this point, Crockett paused, aghast. True, most of the garrison were now retiring to the fort in good order, but the lack of all preparation was painfully evident. Upon reaching the walls, they fell into wild disorder. Everyone gave orders, no one obeyed them. Men who had sold muskets and rifles for liquor, were yelling for weapons. Others were rushing about or trying to load the cannon, of whose use they knew nothing. Women and children were being hurried into the chapel.

Crockett threaded his way through the tumult to the south battery, where his equipment had been left. There he found Captain Ward, an Irishman, whom he had drunk under the table the preceding night. With a score of men, Ward had his guns loaded and was calmly awaiting orders. Crockett got rifle and powder horn, and grinned at Ward.

"Howdy, Cap'n! By gum, if you ain't sober! First time I've seen you so."

"True for you, Colonel," and the other chuckled. "Devil and

all, I ran out of whiskey just at the proper time, eh? Hello! There's Bowie."

ORDER BEGAN to come out of the chaos. Bowie, who disputed the command with Travis, took a detachment and began to scour the nearer houses of the town in search of food. Another squad was rounding up cattle and driving them into one of the enclosures. Travis, redheaded, feverish, resolute, began whipping the men into shape and seeing to the guns.

The afternoon wore on. Into Bexar were pouring dragoons and engineers and infantry of Santa Anna. Apparently an endless stream of them. A burst of music from regimental bands and volleys of cheering tokened the arrival of El Presidente himself. As evening approached, dragoons came galloping close. Travis ordered Captain Ward to fire his eighteen-pounder at the enemy. The cannon crashed out.

Later, a number of horsemen rode toward the fort, bugle blowing and a white flag raised. Travis, who was in the battery with Crockett, shook his head at those around.

"Ignore it, ignore it!" he exclaimed hotly. "If they want to parley, let 'em come to the gate and be admitted—what the devil!"

From the side entrance, where Bowie commanded the barracks and batteries off to the right, a party of men were leaving the fort with a white flag. Travis cursed, then fell silent. He was in command of the troops of the alleged Texas government. Bowie was the idol of the volunteers. One had been placed in command of Bexar by the Convention, which was anti-Houston, and the other had been unanimously elected by the garrison. For the past two weeks, both factions had been engaged in a heated quarrel over authority.

When the white flag returned, the message from the Mexicans was simple. Surrender at discretion as rebels—which meant execution. Already, no quarter had been proclaimed. The red flag blowing at the tower of San Fernando church, in the town, announced it. The alternative was to fight—or run.

EVENING. IN the great open courtyard in front of the chapel and behind the main batteries, Crockett looked on with his shrewd, patient eyes as the garrison assembled. Among the volunteers were Captain Seguin and other Mexicans. There were Negro slaves. There were women. Bowie was surrounded by his wild fighters; Travis by his more disciplined men. The two leaders conferred and shook hands. Bowie, a dark flush in his features, a feverish glitter in his bright blue eyes, waved an arm.

"All right, boys!" he lifted his voice. "Travis is in command. Take his orders!"

A wild joyous yell pealed up. The common peril had ended all dissension. Travis was an accomplished, even dramatic, speaker, and harangued the garrison briefly. The Mexican troops and batteries had spread out, but on the east side were none. The garrison could get away. A man was taking out dispatches. All could leave if they so desired.

"We've plenty of powder," he concluded. "Fannin has three hundred men at Goliad, and can join us. The government can get an army here if we give 'em time. Fight or run?"

He was answered by a tumultuous roar. Fight!

"By thunder," lifted the whimsical voice of Davy Crockett, "I sure hope Santy Anny comes a-piling in! If somebody will grease him, I'll guarantee to swaller him, head, horns and all."

There was a rollicking burst of laughter.

Next morning the news spread that Jim Bowie was down with some kind of fever. The Mexican townfolk who sought refuge here, had sneaked home during the night. Ten of their women remained in the chapel, and one of these, Andrea Candelaria, took her place as nurse for Bowie, who was moved into an upper room of the barracks.

The cannon had begun to thunder.

Nine batteries in all were planted, and now Davy Crockett began to enjoy himself. The Mexicans attempted no assault, but Crockett led out parties of skirmishers by day and night. An uninterrupted rain of shell, ball and bombs was maintained upon the devoted group of buildings; not a man inside was killed, but a huge breach was laid open at the northeast angle, the roofs were riddled, the walls smashed in.

Better than the cannon that made reply, were the rifles. Crockett was deadly at this work, bringing down man after man about the Mexican pieces. The besieged were by this time jesting at the cannon which killed nobody, but Colonel Travis knew better. His messengers went forth to Fannin, to Houston, to the Convention, for aid. Jim Bowie lay upon the bed from which he would never rise, being delirious with pneumonia and nursed constantly by the faithful Andrea Candelaria, He would meet death in a woman's arms—as had been foretold him ere this.

THE 29TH of February. That night Captain Seguin, with his Mexican orderly, rode through the fire of the dragoons, in a desperate attempt to bring Fannin to the rescue. Next night, thirty-two men from Gonzales rode in, with Colorado Smith guiding them. Smith turned around and departed two nights later, taking the last word from Travis.

"I have held this place ten days . . . and I shall continue to hold it till I get relief from my countrymen, or I will perish in the attempt."

No bombast there; the old dramatic Travis was stilled. Perhaps the calm, shrewd genius of Crockett helped him write those words. The men from Gonzales had told the worst— Houston was desperately trying to rally men and could not. Another Mexican column was holding Fannin in check. One hundred and eighty-three men now, within the walls, and thousands around them under the blood-red flag that still drooped from the high church tower. There was no doubt of the issue.

"I reckon," drawled Crockett, "that as long as we can enjoy a dram o' liquor and keep plugging away at them 'tarnal Mexicans yonder, we're safe enough behind these walls. Safer, anyhow, than if we tried to skedaddle!"

Bonham came in next night, too—chivalrous Bonham, with definite news that there was no relief, and no hope. Day and night, the cannon were smashing away. Bonham rode in through the enemy, knowing he came to a certain ending here. Crockett struck hands with him quickly, harshly, gladly; and together Tennessee and South Carolina enjoyed a horn of liquor to the safe arrival.

Two tentative attacks, mere feelers toward assault, had been repulsed.

On the night of the fifth, Crockett heard the word that Bowie was dying. He went to the upper room and sat there for a time to relieve the nurse. Bowie was conscious, but weak. Not too weak to lift his brass pistols, however. He had Davy Crockett load them and leave them on his cot, and fell asleep again.

A damp, misty night. In the cattle enclosure where the men bivouacked in shelter from the cannon balls, Crockett came down in time to help barbecue some meat and get his share of it. They had counted thirty corpses that day, lying out around the main Mexican battery, and Crockett came in for hearty congratulations.

A MIXED lot, these shadowy figures crowded about the fires. Irish, Scotch, French, English, German, Dane, Mexican; cobblers, army men, adventurers, settlers, Indian fighters, store clerks, gentlemen. Crockett's droll stories set them all to laughing, and after a time he departed to his cot in the officers' quarters, between the chapel and the barracks. In the room overhead lay Bowie.

"How's Betsy behaving?" demanded Bonham jocularly, coming in to retire. Crockett glanced at his rifle and grunted.

"Oh, me and Betsy are still friends, I reckon. I'm itching to get me a shot at one o' them gold-laced officers, suh."

"Maybe you will yet," and Bonham laughed as he drew off his boots. "By the way, Travis wants you to relieve him at midnight, in charge of the guard. He'll wake you."

"Fine and dandy," said Crockett, with a nod. "Then I'll snooze off. 'Night!"

He turned his back to the light and was asleep almost at once.

Midnight. An occasional cannon sent its load tearing into the buildings. Travis, when Crockett joined him, peered out anxiously at the lights of the batteries and the town, and shook his head.

"Keep a sharp eye, Colonel. A good many lights have been bobbing around out there. They may try to make another night assault, though I doubt it."

"You bet I'll keep awake," and Crockett chuckled. "Ain't anxious to get my scalp lifted, not by a good deal! Sleep tight."

Only trained frontier senses could make anything of a damp, murky night like this. The river-mist reeked up and hid the stars, though not thickly enough to cast any fog around the buildings. From the parapet, Crockett listened, took a dram now and then to keep out the cold, chatted with the sentries. The hours drew on. The voices of women praying came at times from the former chapel, and the voices of wounded men.

To the left of this chapel and its barricaded courtyard in front, rose the barracks. Out in front of all these, across the open space, lay the main breastworks, the cannon. There at the northeast corner was the breach, wide open to assault. This breach, however, was commanded by the artillery to either side.

Dawn lifted and stirred. A man wakened Travis, shaking him.

"Look alive, Cunnel? Cunnel Crockett allows you'd better step out."

A WORD to Bonham, and Travis was gone, buckling on his tunic. He found Crockett in the dawn-darkness.

"What's up?"

"Troops a-moving, I reckon," drawled the man from Tennessee. "If I was you, I'd rouse all hands—"

A crash came from the nearest Mexican battery, re-echoed from the barracks roof as the ball tore through, showering stone and plaster about. Ward's voice broke from the darkness. The red roar of his gun made instant response. Gun for gun.

"Look alive, boys!" Travis started the word. "Every man to his post."

Crockett sauntered away to the battery in front of the chapel, exchanged a jest with Ward, shared a last dram with him. Then to work loading Betsy.

Movement out there, no mistake about it; the movement of companies and regiments tramping along. From the walls came the *tamp-tamp* of ramrods tapped down, as rifles and muskets were loaded. Low voices rose from about the cannon. Crockett waited, immobile, leaning on his rifle, coonskin cap shoved back on his head.

Tension grew and grew, so that men fell silent, staring into the darkness. They could feel it now, could sense the gathering forces, the coming of the moment.

"Think they're coming, Cunnel?" one of the men exclaimed.

"I reckon," said Crockett calmly. "Give 'em hell, boys, when they do!"

Murmurs, reassuring, stout-hearted, made response. The darkness was thinning out now. Things began to take shape in the grayness. Then, sudden as death, a clear silvery bugle lifted a quick double-step note. Cheers made answer—a wild chorus of voices out in the grayness.

"*Viva Mexico! Viva El Presidente!*"

"Let 'em have it!" shouted Travis.

Things were moving—masses of things. Rifles barked here and there. The cannon began to roar. The cheers changed to yells, to screams. Crockett waited. Three columns—one of them here, coming straight at the walls. A storm of musketry burst forth on all sides; bullets sang and whistled, chipped the stones, brought men down to death.

Crockett lifted his long rifle. He saw now the thing he had

waited this long while, the gaudy figure surrounded by aides. Santa Anna himself? Perhaps; his finger pressed the trigger. Not Santa Anna, but another.

SUDDEN, UPON the roar and banging and shouting, grew a great burst of music from the Mexican battery by the bridge, five hundred yards away. All Santa Anna's massed bands were there, and into the dawn the brazen throats trumpeted out the *deguello*—the "no quarter" music, played for generations at bullfights when the bull was about to die. Now it was no bull dying.

As though in response, the cannon along the walls belched smoke and grape into the masses below. The dawn was clearing fast; men could see to shoot. Crockett was firing as rapidly as he could load, picking off the officers. The column below was halted, smashed, repulsed. It broke up and flooded out around the walls—no more cannon now. The Mexicans were under the walls, too close to reach.

"Smashed 'em, by God!" yelled somebody, exultantly.

But from the north came shouts that fetched Crockett around, aghast. Travis dead! Yells burst out on all sides. The Mexicans were pouring in at the breach, flooding into the courtyard; they had taken the outer barricade and the guns. Bayonets out, muskets spitting—

"Back, everybody!" yelled Crockett.

Full daylight coming rapidly. The Mexican columns were everywhere, over the outer walls; the defenders fell back to the buildings. Crockett gained the twelve-cannonade on the west wall, and found men loading it.

"Let 'em have it!" he ordered, helping them swing it around. Below, the Mexicans were filling the whole courtyard. The carronade belched and roared, the stones shook. A terrible scream rose from those massed victims below.

"Keep it up, boys!" panted Crockett, and caught up his rifle.

They began to load and ram, while a hail of bullets flitted around them. Others came up and joined them. The range of barracks was turned into a hell. The cursing Texians, broken and shattered, filled the rooms, were on the walls—rifles sending death into the Mexican ranks filling the courtyard. Again the carronade roared forth, and again shrieks arose at its voice.

CROCKETT SAW a gun being wheeled from the outer work. He dropped the officer in command; another took his place. The gun was loaded and discharged. Its ball smashed into the first room of the barracks, burst down the doors. Hard upon it flooded Mexicans, a solid mass of them pouring in upon the barracks room. Shots, the glint of knives, wild yells and a swirling of men for a little space; then the bayonets were red. Again the cannon smashed forth at the next room—no communication here.

Crockett was turned half-around, staggered, caught himself. Half the men were dead, here around the carronade. As he rammed home the charge in his rifle, blood was running from his sleeve. The carronade belched once more, and once more shrieks welled up from the mass of troops below—but this was the last time. Balls hailed around. The Mexicans were up on the roofs now, clearing them, bayonets flashing. The men around the carronade wilted and drooped and died.

With a leap, Crockett was gone. His eagle eye perceived that everything was lost; the last stand would come by the chapel. As he left the roof, he saw Dickinson, with his child in his arms, leap from the east wall for the irrigation ditch below—leap, and be mowed down by a storm of musketry. He and the child both.

Then Crockett was gone from the wall, gone to the old chapel. His rifle spoke there for a little while, as rapidly as might be.

In the upper room of the officers' quarters, the savage swart faces blocked in at the door and halted. Bowie lay there in bed, his blue eyes glittering, his pistols lifting; they fired, as Andrea Candelaria shrieked in horror. She shrieked at her own people, these Mexicans. She flung herself forward, caught the head of

Bowie in her arms, tried to shield him with her own body. A musket roared. The bullet drew blood from her chin, passed on into Bowie's heart.

Men surged in. They tore her away, tore the dead thing from the cot, lifted it on their bayonets and so passed it out and hurled it into the courtyard below. The cannon was crashing again. A room crowded with wounded men; a blast of grape tore through doors and walls and flesh, and when the soldiers burst in there were few to feel the bayonet.

CLEARED, NOW. A few men on the chapel roof, others in the chapel. From the battery by the bridge, Santa Anna and his staff advanced. The men on the roof fired right willingly, and balls whistled, so that El Presidente scampered back in all haste. And, above everything, the shrill music of the *deguello* pealed unto heaven, its reiterant refrain maddening the blood.

Crockett fired methodically, mechanically, carefully, dropping only officers. Men he knew well were sprawled in death, or writhing in agony. Closer now, all of them, swarthy Mexicans, alert graceful officers—he killed them very neatly. The fighting was drawing near him. He retreated into a corner of the embrasures, and a few men with him. The old doors of the former chapel were shut and barred. Across the courtyard, he saw Ward's gun being wheeled around and loaded. Not by Ward; the happy Irishman lay across the parapet.

Five or six Mexicans clumped together—Mexicans of the garrison, fighting with all the ferocity of the Texians, knife aflash and defiance on their lips. Never a whine for mercy. An officer and a score of soldiers came at them with the bayonet. Crockett grimaced and dropped the officer in his tracks. The bayonets plunged and plunged again, and the little clump was gone, still stabbing for a space, then sprawled in death.

Bullets buzzing like bees all around. Crockett dashed blood out of his eyes. His? No time to think about that. Five or six men around him now, rifles reloading, faces grim, eyes staring death in the face. Then a cannon-blast—Ward's cannon, full at the chapel doors. They splintered under the hurtling iron, splintered and crashed and gaped. A howling flood of soldiery went at them, burst them in.

Screams from the chapel. The women were not hurt. Crockett had one wild glimpse of Major Evans, lighted match in hand, rushing for the powder magazine. Then Evans was down, hit. He struggled to one knee. Half a dozen bayonets darted into him all at once, and the magazine was not fired.

A white thing out there in the courtyard, lifted on the bayonets of blood-mad soldiers. A white thing, mangled and ripped. That had been Jim Bowie.

"By God, give 'em hell!" yelled Crockett in a sudden spasm of unleashed ferocity. The little knot of men around him echoed the yell. The rifles barked out—the last shot. Stark berserk rage fell upon them all, gripped them up in a whirlwind. Half-a-dozen wounded men were dragged out of the old chapel and butchered on the stones.

"See you in hell, Davy—here they come!" rang a shout.

A sudden rushing wave of them, swart, sweating faces, white teeth, staring eyes, bayonets a-glitter—a wave that crested upward over the heaps of corpses and broke. The long rifles fell and smashed. The iron barrels fell and fell again. The wave was shattered, it fell back in wild fear and terror of these flailing demons. Five left on their feet.

Knives out now. Bowie knives, hunting knives, as the ring of bayonets hurtled in over the corpses. Five of them in a corner of the wall. Two or three up on the roof, shooting straight down into the heads of the Mexicans. Bullets swept the roof and they were silent. Five left here in the swirling tide of uniforms, breaking them, stabbing in dread silence, stabbing against the long bayonets. Breaking them again, by the Lord! Breaking them, until the Mexicans yelled in sudden panic that these were devils, not men, and drew back.

Three on their feet now, hands and arms red, knives red, silent. The bayonets drew back and back. An officer cracked out orders. Crockett stooped, caught the barrel of his rifle, and with one swing sent it at the squad—a last gesture of flying iron that struck down a man.

The muskets crashed. Inside the ring of corpses, only corpses were left.

Music swirled higher and higher. Yells and cheers rang out. "*El Presidente! Viva! Viva Santa Anna!*"

HE CAME, slender, gold-laced, erect, his glittering staff around him; came now, when bullets flew no more. Short, sharp orders. Among the heaps of death, wounded men were brought forth, and the bayonets became red again, stabbing them anew. All of them, without mercy. No quarter to these rebels!

A sudden burst of shouts, of wild yells. A swirl of men staggering out all in a knot, then disintegrating. Half-a-dozen Texians found in a room somewhere. An officer saluted El Presidente, asked for their lives.

"You have your orders. Obey them."

The muskets crashed again, for the last volley.

The women were brought out. El Presidente bowed to them gracefully, saluted them, shrugged at sight of the two negroes— body servants of Bowie and Travis. Andrea Canderalia, with blood on her chin, drew his curious glance for an instant. But it was diverted by excited yells, a streaming hurry of soldiers— a handful of the rebels found somewhere. The yells died out in hysteric laughter as the red beyonets drove down.

More wounded. A few men outside, who had jumped from the walls. They were hunted down with shout and jeer. Now a search was begun for any other survivors.

The sun was just rising. It was thirty-two minutes from the time the first signal bugle had sounded the assault.

El Presidente sent for his negro cook, Ben, who knew most of the Texian leaders by sight. With his aide, Almonte, he had Ben move about among the dead, displaying the corpses and picking out those of the leaders. Terrified, shaking, the frightened negro identified Travis, then the mangled body of Bowie.

Then in the southwest corner he pointed to a bullet-riddled thing in blood-smeared fringed leather garments.

El Presidente looked, and turned away with a shrug.

"El Coronel Crockett?" he repeated. "There must be some mistake. I never heard of him. He is not of Texas, eh? Come, Almonte; it's time for breakfast. The breakfast of victory!"

"Another such victory," said Almonte in a low voice, "and we are ruined."

THE SUN rose higher, the full day sprang into life. The dead were sorted out and laid aside; the Mexican dead, for burial. The wounded were carried to hastily constructed shelters along the river—the Mexican wounded.

As the day wore on, a few more survivors turned up—some men hiding in a loft, a man who had gained an irrigation ditch and shelter of a bridge there. The volleys rang out once again; the bodies were pitched into the courtyard with the rest. The place was looted of arms and aught else that could be worth while.

Wood was gathered from near and far. Wood from field and forest, wood from the shattered barracks, beams from the breached defenses, old black oak from the organ-loft in the former chapel. Three great piles grew up, piles of bodies and of wood intermingled.

Santa Anna came again to the scene of his conquest and watched the work go forward. Here was the last gesture of contempt, of insult toward rebels. He examined the wounds of these dead men with curious interest. Two soldiers lifted a white mangled thing that El Presidente recognized. He checked the men.

"Wait," he said irresolutely. "Wait. Señor Bowie—he was too brave a man to be burned like a dog. He should have burial."

He caught the curious stares of his staff. What! A moment of weakness in the conqueror? Santa Anna read the looks aright, and irritation seized upon him. He turned away with a shrug.

"Well, never mind; throw him in."

The three piles grew and grew until all was done and the torch applied. Three columns of smoke blended and lifted into the sky. They swung in the eddying breeze and then were caught and carried toward the Mexican camp, with a splutter of sparks and a rain of fiery particles.

And the Mexicans, some of them, looked up with terrified eyes and crossed themselves. An omen, they muttered; an evil omen.

They were right. While these men died and were burned, the Convention had at last declared for independence. The die was cast. Texas was no longer a part of Mexico.

V

LOSER PAYS

ONE bitter cold, dark night my car broke down, just outside Goliad. Storm, rain and sweeping wind. A passing motorist agreed to send help. I waited, and while the wind howled, I thought of the day, a hundred years ago, when three brush fires had crackled close by here. A distant shouting came down the wind—the voices of many men—yet no one was in sight. The voices died out, and then the slow but indescribably dignified voice of one man singing reached me. A gallant, rich voice, and the words came clearer and clearer:

"We asked and we gave no quarter. When we shot, we shot to kill.
And never a one of us whimpered when we had to foot the bill.
From Trinity to Laredo, by prairie and Alamo
We paid with our lives for Texas, a *hundred* years ago."

A burst of thin and distant yells swooped down with the wind, and after it a quick, fierce shout in unison:

"Here's to you, Colonel Fannin, damn your eyes!"

Was it real? I blinked around, shivered, found and saw nothing; yet it seemed that there came another burst of yells, and the rushing tumult of hoofbeats passing overhead. Here by the Coleto river men had fought like heroes, had died like heroes for the sake of other men—

IMPETUOUS, ARDENT, chivalric, the young Geor-

gian leaped to his feet. The others looked at him expectantly. He had already won a dashing repute, had Fannin. He had fought beside Jim Bowie, had proved his ability to lead men. In this new year of 1835, great things were expected from him.

"If Santa Anna is really coming with the whole army of Mexico," he cried, "then don't let him set foot on Texan soil! Strike ahead of him. Straight across the hundred and fifty miles of desert lies Matamoras. Strike there! An expedition can take and hold it. Santa Anna will be cut off from the sea. He'll have deserts behind him. Carry the war into Mexico, and save Texas!"

San Felipe went wild with delight.

For, at San Felipe was assembled the convention of Texas, now in rebellion. It was no secret that Santa Anna, the dictator, was somewhere on the march north with the overwhelming forces of Mexico. Carry the war into Mexico! Capture Matamoras!

Colonel Fannin was, on the instant, given unexampled

powers. Although Houston was the general, Fannin was made practically independent. He was sent hot-foot to take command of Goliad, raise men and supplies, and then march on Matamoras. Colonel Johnson and Doctor Grant were to take post at San Patricio, gather horses, and then unite with Fannin in his march. All this by the council. And nothing doubting, Fannin departed, eager and ardent.

But at San Felipe reigned dissension.

Governor Smith—for as yet Texas had no thought of seceding from Mexico—had been elected to office; and in no time he was at open war with the council. Sam Houston was appointed general, deposed, appointed again. He stuck with the governor, the mainspring of authority. Colonel Travis was sent to command at Bexar, or San Antonio, with a small force. Fannin, at Goliad, had four hundred men. Johnson and Grant had another hundred.

Although none of them knew it, Santa Anna was even then almost upon them.

In San Felipe, matters went from bad to worse. The governor accused the council of graft and playing politics; the council went to work to depose him, and eventually did it. But first— who was to be obeyed? Houston ordered Travis to abandon Bexar, blow up the Alamo, and fall back to a prepared line of defence. The council sent post-haste orders to do no such thing but hold the Alamo.

And Fannin was at Goliad, preparing for the march on Matamoras. Suddenly the council revoked all orders to him. He was left to his own resources. And like a whirlwind, Santa Anna came when least expected. A new convention was meeting, Houston was at last in supreme command—too late. The agony of Goliad had begun. News was slow to travel in that day.

FEBRUARY DREW on apace. With Fannin was Major William Ward and his Georgia Battalion—a hundred volunteers who had come West to free Texas, only to find that so far Texas did not want to be freed. They had hailed Fannin jubilantly, they obeyed him with fanatic devotion.

"Ward, we're up a stump," said Fannin despondently, huddling one evening over a fire with his friend. It was the 25th of February. "No word from San Patricio, and if Johnson and Grant don't find horses for us, we can't strike at Matamoras. Where Santa Anna is, nobody knows. Who's in command, nobody knows."

"It's a sweet mess," commented Ward. "Looks like all we can do is hang on and see what turns up. Queer we don't get some news from San Patricio."

Fannin nodded. "I feel incompetent, and that's the truth. I've asked the council to relieve me of command; I'm no soldier, and know it. Houston is the man of the hour, whether I like him or not. But, damn it, what can I do? They order me not to retreat. Houston has sent no orders at all. The governor has forbidden the Matamoras expedition, the council says to go ahead. I'm just no soldier, that's all. I can command a company, but I'm not the man to hold a chief command—"

"Good God, man! Nobody could, under such circumstances!" exploded Ward. "Why, the situation is utterly insane! Suppose Santa Anna should show up now?"

A sharp rap at the door. An orderly entered. Outside was a rising buzz of voices.

"Courier from Bexar, Colonel."

An exhausted, excited man stumbled into the room, thrusting out a letter. Fannin leaped up at sight of his face.

"What is it? What's happened?"

"Santy Anny—him and the hull damned Mexican army! Thousands of 'em. Travis has took to the Alamo, wants you to come a-running."

Fannin tore at the letter. He heard one low-voiced, tragic oath from Ward, as they were alone again. Then he extended the letter in silent dismay. Ward read it and looked up. Their eyes met for a moment in mutual comprehension.

"Well, it's come." Fannin squared his shoulders. "Half our men here are out foraging for food. We've no horses, only a few oxen for the wagons and artillery. We've one tierce of beef—and nothing else. Travis wants us to bring our artillery and ammunition and come to lend a hand."

"It's impossible!" said Ward. "And Matamoras—"

"Matamoras be damned—that's all washed up now. I'll send Johnson word to fall back here and join us. Get a courier ready while I write the letter, will you? Then we'll have to round up our men and try to get some transport."

Travis—holding the Alamo to death! The thought burned.

And yet, despite every effort, Fannin could not get off until three days later; then his transport broke down within a quarter-mile. To move the ammunition and cannon was impossible. His scouts brought in word of Mexican dragoons. To reach Bexar, a hundred miles away, was simply an impossibility. Travis had been ordered by Houston to blow up the Alamo and fall back; the council had sternly countermanded this order. To know what was going on, was out of the question. Fannin returned to Goliad and fell to work at his defences. His men were ragged, barefoot, starving. He wrote the council in words of desperate gallantry:

"I again repeat that I consider myself bound to await your orders, I have orders from you to await reinforcements. I am desirous to be erased from the list of officers and have leave to bring off my brave volunteers in the best manner I may be able."

THEN, LIKE a thunderbolt, came the news that General Urrea had destroyed the force at San Patricio. Johnson and four of his men alone escaped; the others were butchered. They had refused to obey the order to join Fannin, and paid the price.

Settlers at the Refugio Mission sent in an appeal for help. Fannin despatched Captain King and a few men to the mission, thirty miles distant, to escort in the settlers. And all this while Travis was holding the Alamo—or was he? A second courier had come in with another urgent request for men and ammunition.

"I can't stand it!" cried Fannin to his friend, striding up and down the room, his features agonized. "To think of Travis and the others there, desperate—and we sit here helpless to lend a hand, helpless to join him! Evidently, Urrea commands a second army of Mexicans pushing up at us. And no orders—nothing! No horses, no reinforcements. I'm sending out parties tomorrow to scour the farms for wagons and oxen. We may pick up a few."

"Hang on," advised Ward grimly. "You've got four hundred men to think about, old chap. Funny we don't get any word from King."

Fannin snorted. "He should have been back with those settlers ere this. I told him to get back instantly. Hang on? Yes, that's all we can do, damn it!"

News burst suddenly. A courier came in with word that the frightened convention had once more placed Sam Houston in command of all Texas forces. Relief would be sent to Travis at once. Orders might be expected by Fannin at once.

None came. Instead, a messenger from King at Refugio begged for help. He had fought off a detachment of Mexican lancers but the mission was surrounded.

"Let me go and bring him in," said Ward. "These boys of mine are itching for a scrap anyhow."

"Go ahead, and God keep you!" said Fannin simply.

The Georgia Battalion, with yelps of delight, fell in. Then eyes went upward; a murmur grew and grew. "The flag! Ain't we taking it?"

Their flag had been raised above the mission—a white flag bearing a blue star and the legend "Liberty Or Death." A flag of silk, presented to the Battalion back in Georgia by a Miss Troutman. Colonel Ward looked up at it, and saluted it gallantly.

"Leave it for luck, boys!" he cried. "We don't need it; and maybe it'll be safer here. Attention!"

Fannin sat tight, perforce, and looked to his defenses. The Alamo had already fallen, but he would be slow to learn of it. Sam Houston, with a relieving force, had been two days too late.

WARD AND his Georgia boys marched the thirty miles to Refugio in rollicking gaity, reached there late on the 13th, and found all well. King had beaten off an attack and the Mexicans had apparently dispersed. Ward now had a hundred and forty men all told.

Next morning, preparing for the return march, his scouts dashed in. Mexicans at hand, and plenty of 'em! Dragoons and lancers on the run!

And on the run they came, a thousand strong, pennons flying and bugles blowing. When they got under the very walls of the mission. Ward's men opened fire. The ranks were shattered and broken. The Mexicans wheeled and departed, only to reform again and again.

Until four in the afternoon, the attacks continued. Then, leaving a couple of hundred dead, the enemy rode off for good. And not one of Ward's command was killed.

That night came in a frantic message from Fannin. Orders at last from Houston; he was to abandon Goliad and retreat, joining Houston on the Guadeloupe. Ward must come in at once with his command. Head for Victoria on the Guadeloupe.

Ward lost not a moment. At midnight he marched out with

his Georgia boys, flushed with victory. Mexican cavalry picked them up with morning, but Ward headed through woods and swamps for the Guadeloupe and threw off the pursuit. Day after day they struggled on. Came the 19th, and the sounds of cannonading from Goliad.

Ward pressed onward, obeying orders. Victoria at last—and Mexican troops there! Cavalry all about him. Urrea's whole army was about him. He was caught.

He went to Urrea's camp. Urrea offered him free passage to New Orleans if he would surrender. Ward took back the word to the Georgia boys and advised against it. Fight to the last ditch! But the dragoons, the lancers, the infantry, the artillery—the Georgia boys lost heart. They voted for surrender. Fannin had been destroyed. They had no hope of fighting through.

They surrendered, and were marched to Goliad.

What of Fannin, meantime—Fannin, undergoing his agony of glorious failure?

On the 14th, an express reached him from Houston, with definite orders to bring off what cannon he could, abandon Goliad, and fall back to the Guadeloupe. He sent messengers to Ward, and had no word back. He buried some of his guns, hastily set about collecting wagons and transport, and waited until the 18th for Ward, in vain.

This day, his scouts brought in word of increasing numbers of Mexican cavalry.

Next morning he marched out, with three hundred men, setting fire to the wooden buildings, with what ammunition he could not take. He had no fear of the Mexicans; with his officers, he laughed at them, for fighting with Bowie had imbued him with the idea that one Texian could disperse a dozen dragoons.

They set forth gaily, then, to join Houston and seek the war. Free Texas! The convention had declared for liberty. The die was cast. To the ardent Fannin, the days of 1776 were come again. He led his men out with cheers. Not a Mexican in sight as they crossed the river at the ford, got the light artillery and the wagons over, and headed across the prairie for Coleto Creek, ten miles away.

No danger anywhere. Eight miles were covered, when it became necessary to rearrange the hasty loads and teams. Two miles distant lay the creek, thickly wooded. The scouts urged Fannin to make his halt there, but he shrugged and gave the orders. Camp was made, the oxen were unyoked from the guns and wagons, were allowed to graze. His little force of mounted men was sent out to scout; that was the last heard from them.

SUDDENLY A yell arose. Fannin leaped to a wagon and looked forth; a shout broke from him, a shout of eagerness, of delight. Mexicans! A few troops of lancers breaking from cover of the trees—only a few troops. And they meant to attack. Good!

The last chance to make the timber was lost.

Swiftly, Fannin drew up his men in hollow square, three rifles deep, the cannon at the four corners. He asked nothing better than a cavalry charge; and he got it. He got more than he bargained for. The lancers deployed, and he eagerly opened on them with his cannon.

Then more lancers appeared. Helmets glittered and drew into sight from the brush. Dragoons! Company on company of them. A wild burst of yells lifted—a company of Indian scouts, sharpshooters, scattering out. A column of infantry advanced.

And suddenly Fannin knew he was caught, there in the open, by Urrea's whole army. Caught and surrounded.

"That's no convict infantry," spoke up a scout. "That's the Tampico regiment, Cunnel—the crack outfit of the hull Mexican force."

"So much the better!" Fannin's gay, wild laugh rang out. If a cold hand laid grip on his heart, none suspected it. "So much the better. Give 'em hell, boys!"

A ragged cheer went up, gained volume, became a bedlam of voices. No surrender!

The cheering died. The dragoons and lancers were spreading out, coming in on three sides, quickening pace. Hands gripped on rifles; the artillerymen hastily loaded with grape and canister. The squadrons were trotting now, pennons flying, lances glittering, escopetas ready for firing. Suddenly a trumpet outblew, then another, and the horses leaped to a gallop. Down came the lances. The charge thundered in upon three sides, brown faces alight with battle-lust, yells rising high.

Then the rifles began to crack. The light cannon crashed out. Horrible lanes of death were opened in those advancing ranks, but they came on. Horses went down, men went down, but the others came on. On and on, until the third and reserve rank of men loosed their fire and vomited death into the broken squadrons. They wheeled and went galloping away, leaving dead and wounded men and horses strewn on the prairie.

They reformed, while the exultant lines of Texians yelled themselves hoarse. Formed up again on three sides. The regiment of Tampico was advancing on the left flank, twelve hundred strong, bayonets glittering, lines dressed as though on parade.

Again the trumpets lifted silvery voices. The squadrons came on at the gallop, the Tampico regiment charged in with the cold steel. Bullets smashed into them. Their ranks were broken, faltered, shaken. They dispersed and flung themselves into the long grass. The cavalry squadrons were shattered anew by that deadly fire. They swerved and galloped away.

Yells redoubled. Fannin, despite that cold grip clutching his heart, despite the blood pouring down from his thigh, yelled with the rest. Then he was forced from his feet and submitted to being bandaged. A severe wound enough, though the bone was not broken. Bandaged, he came up again, leaning on a rifle. They greeted him with cheers and yells of delight.

Another charge. The Tampico regiment in the grass was

joined by the Indian sharpshooters. No more charges for them; but as the cavalry swept in, their bullets hailed into the hollow square of riflemen.

Then, with men dying and wounded, the rifles turned to the grass fighters. Grape searched them out, deadly bullets found them. A few of the Indian scouts remained, but the rest broke and fled. Evening was coming down, and the battle of the Coleto was won for Texas.

I N T H E dusk, Fannin assembled the men around him. Exultation had gone. He faced them level-eyed, white-lipped, calmly. That cold clutch had fastened tight upon his heart now, but his voice was gay and ringing as ever.

"Boys, the decision is up to you now," he declared. "We've licked them. Maybe we can lick them again. We've got a right smart of wounded men to think about, and mighty little water in camp. We can't hope for any reinforcements—what's become of Ward and the Georgia boys, nobody knows. More than likely, there'll be fresh Mexican troops here by morning."

The sober, deadly words drove into them. The men listened, staring at him as he leaned on his rifle-crutch in the gathering dusk.

"Face the facts," he went on. "Our wagons have broken down. We've no way to carry off any wounded men. If we leave them here, they'll be butchered. You heard the yells of no quarter! Now, we've got to make our choice and make it quick. We can abandon the wounded, the artillery, the baggage, and break through them for the Guadeloupe. We can do it with one smash; we've licked them already. Or else we can throw up entrenchments and lick them again if we have to do it. We've mighty little water, remember. The powder has run out. We've got about two charges for each cannon left."

He paused, compressed his lips for a moment, then went on.

"I'm giving no orders," came his voice, slowly. "I'll do whatever the majority decides is best. If you so decide, I'll stay with the other wounded men and order you on. I'll say frankly that by morning we'll probably find twice as many Mexicans here, and your one chance is to break 'em now and—"

"To hell with 'em!" yelled a frontiersman suddenly. "Hey, Cunnel! You mean to say we got to leave the wounded here to be butchered?"

"There's nothing else for it," Fannin rejoined. "It's better that a few should die, than that all hands should take the risk."

"Be damned if we do!" rose the shrill yell of indignation. It was echoed and reechoed by the thronged circle of men. "We stay right here!"

Fannin put it to the vote. Not one dissenting voice was raised.

"I'm proud of you, boys'." rang out his clarion words. "Then get to work and throw up trenches and let 'em come and be damned!" With a burst of cheers, the wearied men fell to work with new enthusiasm. But the wounded men cried for water.

FANNIN LAY blanket-wrapped in the darkness; no fires, for the Indian snipers were still at work. His wound stiffened. Worse than his wound, was the agony of his soul. He had done what he could; all that any man can do. Circumstances had hemmed him in, beaten him back, crushed him down. Victorious, he looked failure in the face and recognized it. He knew what the morrow must bring forth, and trembled; not for himself, but for these three hundred men around him.

This night, he aged twenty years. As the hours crept toward dawn, he knew the worst. The rumble of artillery lifted along the ground, the measured tread of fresh cavalry squadrons shook the long quivering grass; but they were not coming to his help. The water had given out ere midnight. The feverish cries of the wounded rang in the darkness, pitifully.

Slowly the dawn broke. A rifle cracked, then another. Silence again, and men were roused from sleep. Fannin stood clutching his rifle-crutch, peering out at the higher ground all about, as the slow day broke. Colder and grimmer grew the grip on his heart. There on the eminence, the hillock he should have seized, rose a gay cluster of horsemen. Officers, a flag. Epaulets, the gay glimmer of uniforms in the sunrise. General Urrea in person and his staff.

Artillery posted now; a battery within six hundred yards of the camp. Fresh squadrons wheeling about, preparing to attack. One of the Mexican guns suddenly belched smoke, and into the camp rained grape.

"Hold your fire," Fannin cautioned his men. "No reply. Save the last powder-charges for their attack."

The Mexican guns crashed and crashed again. Suddenly their fire ceased. An officer and a man with a white flag appeared, riding in. Fannin sent Major Wallace out to meet them. Terms were offered; surrender at discretion. Major Wallace laughed.

"Before we'll yield on such terms," rang out his voice, "we'll fight as long as there's a man left to fire a gun!"

The officer went galloping toward the hillock. The squadrons formed up for attack, with trumpets shrilling. Then, abruptly, General Urrea himself with his staff came riding toward the camp, white flag displayed.

"Come on, Wallace," said Fannin. "Give me a hand and we'll say howdy to him."

He struggled out into the open. Urrea dismounted, greeted him with gallant words.

"There has been enough bloodshed, Colonel Fannin. Surrender, and I'll grant you honorable terms. Your freedom on parole, if you like."

SUDDEN RELIEF flooded into Fannin. Urrea was afraid to face those rifles again; the pompous boast of "no quarter to rebels!" was a thing of the past. They were saved, all of them.

"Will you come into our camp?" he asked. "It is difficult for me to stand. We may then reduce the terms to writing, if my men accept."

Urrea assented, called his secretary, and both of them walked into the camp with Fannin and Wallace.

The riflemen stared. For the first time, they saw a Mexican

general at close quarters; gold-laced uniform, high collar, clanking sabre. Then word spread of the proffered terms. Their lives and freedom, on parole. They would be sent back to New Orleans. A cheer arose, and swept along the lines.

The terms were put into writing, both Spanish and English. Fannin read the latter to his men; they approved with a shout. Arms were stacked, water was fetched from the river for the wounded. The Mexicans had horses in plenty; these were hitched to the wagons in which the wounded lay, and with an escort of dragoons, Fannin and his men were marched back to Goliad.

As they went, they saw a courier go streaking off for Bexar. They already had heard from the Mexicans that the Alamo had fallen, and Santa Anna was in command of the town. At the moment, this meant nothing to Fannin. Tortured by his wound, yet immeasurably relieved that the stress was over and his men safe, he thought of nothing else. He could relax at last.

With evening, he and his men were back in the quarters they had abandoned; but now as prisoners, confined and guarded.

Next day arrived a weary, gaping train of prisoners. A Major Miller and eighty men, volunteers from New Orleans to help free Texas; they had come by sea, and landed at Copano to find themselves Mexican prisoners. They were marched in and mingled with Fannin's men. Next morning, however, they were assigned quarters to themselves, and each man of them was bound about the left arm with a white cloth.

"Why?" demanded Fannin, when Major Wallace told him of this.

"Some whim of the Mexicans," and Wallace shrugged. "This Colonel Portilla, who's in command here, is a brute. By the way, I've news of Ward. He'll be here tomorrow."

"Ward! Here?" Fannin raised up on one elbow, then fell back. "Oh, I see. How many of the Georgia boys are left?"

"Most of them, thank heaven! They got the same terms we

did. But our men have all been moved into the old church; they're crowded in and given mighty poor food."

Fannin protested to the commandant, without avail.

Ward, and his weary, despondent men came in next day under guard. Three hundred and fifty prisoners crowded into the old church walls now, poorly fed, yet overjoyed with everything. They had come through victorious, and now they were heading back for New Orleans. Nothing else mattered! And the Mexicans were, in general, friendly enough. Good fellows, after their own fashion.

CAME SATURDAY night, and Fannin had his cot carried into the church among his men. There was singing and high jubilation all around. A ship was already at Copano to take them away, spread the rumor. Then, as Fannin was carried back again to his own quarters, there was a rush of hoof beats outside the gates, the challenge of a sentinel, the sharp response.

"*Courier from El Presidente!*"

Orders from Santa Anna had arrived, detailed, precise orders from the conqueror of the Alamo. Colonel Portilla had but to obey.

Palm Sunday, the 27th of March. The Mexican forces had swept lower Texas clear of rebels. Santa Anna himself was now pressing on from Bexar, with nothing to stop him but a contemptible, hastily raised little army commanded by Houston, who was in full retreat. The convention, the politicians, the lawyers, the whole government, were in hasty flight for Louisiana and safety.

The men crowded in the church were wakened and ordered out. Squads of them were marched away in three directions as workmen. Three columns were made up. One was marched out under heavy escort on the Bexar road.

"Going to slaughter beeves, señores," said one of the Mexican officers. "Plenty to eat for all today!"

Another column of a hundred on the Copano road; a ship was there, and they were to be started for New Orleans at once.

The third column, south across the prairie—Santa Anna was coming to occupy Goliad and a new camp had to be formed. So they were told. All the officers were here save Fannin. Three hundred and fifty men.

All three columns sighted huge piles of brush being gathered by the working squads.

Coming to the brush piles, each column was formed in a double rank and ordered to sit down on the ground. The men obeyed, in no little wonder at the whole thing. One of them looked around. Suddenly he knew, they all knew, why Miller's men, who were not with them, wore the white arm-bands.

"By God, boys, they're killing us!" rang out the shout.

The muskets began to crash in volleys.

MANY OF the victims survived that first hail of lead in the back. Some tried to fight. Some broke away, and were run down and spitted on cavalry lances. A few gained the shelter of brush and eventually escaped—a scant few. Bullet and lance did their work, and then the bodies were gathered and flung into the gathered brush.

The troops marched back. Now the wounded were dragged forth, and butchered with short shrift. And all the while, Fannin, alone, waited for the death that his guard informed him was coming. Alone—in a sudden horrible burst of realization that would have shaken the sanity of most men.

They aided him out to the square. He hobbled to a bench as ordered, and sat there, and looked up with cool, brave eyes at the officer who brought a white bandage for his eyes.

"Here, Señor Capitan," and he produced his gold watch, "is my watch. As a favor from one soldier to another, will you see that it reaches my wife?"

"But yes, my Coronel," and the officer caught the watch avidly. Fannin reached up and took the bandage.

"I'll put this on myself. Will you see that I'm shot in the heart and not in the head?"

Glib promises. The firing squad stood ready. Fannin's gaze drifted around in the sunlight for one moment; then he reached up and tied the bandage.

"Fire!"

The volley was directed at his head. He was killed instantly, and his body flung into an arroyo outside the fort.

Torches were set to the three piles of brush outside town, after the bodies had been plundered and stripped. Three columns of smoke and crackling flame, that only half did their appointed work. Weeks afterward, when vengeance had run its course and Houston's men had done their work, fragments of charred flesh and bones were picked up near and far—such as the dogs and vultures had left for the finding.

The Alamo had sent up its smoking pyre. Goliad sent up its three trails of smoke. The losers had paid.

But the game was not yet finished.

VI

THE MAN ALONE

I REACHED the old battlefield of San Jacinto about noon. The Texas sun was hot, a hot breeze swept up from the Gulf; just as on that day a hundred years ago when Sam Houston gave the word to charge. The scene fascinated me, not so much for what had happened here, but for what lay behind it. One man, who had prepared against what never came, and who suddenly seized the fleeting moment and grasped immortality. As I stared across the scene, a lilt of song came to me; it waved in the whispering of the grass and trees, it drifted down the hot sunlight. A man's rough, hoarse voice singing, as though to himself, in throaty exultation:

> "We had to win or go under. We fought for a living Cause,
> Not for a passel of statesmen working their slobbering jaws;
> We planted with powder and bullet, we made a republic grow—
> For by God, sir! We founded Texas a hundred years ago!"

I blinked around. Nothing in sight. No one was here. Yet a sudden thin burst of sound lifted, like the thin and distant voices of men in unison roaring forth a wild and hearty yell:

> "Here's to you, Gin'ral Houston, damn your eyes!"

Sheer fancy, of course. And yet this ground had been stained deep with the blood of men; yonder river had run scarlet with death, a hundred years ago—

GONZALES, WHICH had witnessed the first shot fired

for Texas liberty, was now witnessing a very different scene.
Sam Houston and his hastily gathered force, marching to the
relief of the Alamo, had halted here. And here the news had
reached them.

Consternation, grief, filled the town and camp. Scouts were
hurriedly sent forth toward Bexar; a pall of mourning lay over
the place. Scarcely a person had not lost friends or relatives in
the Alamo. Houston sat with Colonel Sherman, the brave Kentuckian who had come to fight for Texas, and despondency
mastered him.

A gaunt man, Houston, massive, powerful, blunt. His deep-set, patient eyes were pools of gray light, deepened by suffering both physical and mental. His gigantic frame wore no uniform, but shabby, baggy, dirty garments. They, like himself, were worn to shreds by what he had endured and spent in the cause of Texas.

"Travis and the rest—all dead!" he growled. "It may not be true. Those two Mexicans who brought the news may have been wrong. We'll hear from Deaf Smith or Karnes or other scouts pretty quick now."

"What'll you do then, Sam?" queried Sherman. He had borne from Kentucky the flag under which the army of Texas marched—a figure of Liberty on a white ground, heavy gold fringe surrounding it.

"God knows!" said Houston. "We've got four hundred men here. I've ordered Fannin to abandon Goliad and fall back to the Guadeloupe. That'll give us four hundred more and some cannon, if he can bring his artillery away. We've got to stop any panic breaking out, or we're done for."

"No panic," said Sherman coolly. "The die is cast now. The Convention has declared for Liberty. We're fighting for freedom, not to keep Texas in the Mexican union. And you're the commander in chief, Sam. They had to come to you at last!"

NO EXULTATION touched the grim bronzed mask of Houston. At last, yes!

All these weary months he had ridden up and down the settlements, preaching liberty, orating, raising men and money. He had been appointed general before, and the politicians gathered at San Felipe had deposed him. They had been fighting among themselves for months in bitter rancor. Mainly, they had been fighting him. They feared his blunt tongue, his vision, his honesty. He was the most powerful man in all Texas, and well they knew it, so the story spread that he wanted to become dictator. He, who had not a dollar nor a home to his name!

Bitterness deepened in his eyes. Two days more, and he would have been in Bexar—but now the Alamo had fallen.

He had four hundred men in his army. How many had come out of Mexico with Santa Anna, no one knew as yet. His army was a pack of volunteers, without discipline. He could give no orders, but only requests. He could punish none. They laughed at any idea of training or order. But they were not laughing tonight, nor was he.

"Sherman, tell me the truth." He lifted the deep gray eyes in a tragic look. "How far can I count on the boys? What do they say about me? I know all that's said of me in San Felipe and so on—but what about the army?"

"They're for you, Sam," said the Kentuckian simply. "They want to fight, and you're the man to lead 'em. All they ask is to meet the Mexicans face to face."

"Yes." The tragic look deepened. Houston's heart sank. "Meet cannon, lancers, trained regiments face to face—with what? Do you know how much artillery, powder and supplies the army has?"

"No," said Sherman in surprise. "Artillery's coming from New Orleans, of course, and I understand there's no lack of transport."

"No lack," said Houston, with a grim smile. "Right now we haven't a cannon. The transport consists of two yoke of oxen, two wagons, and a dozen horses. The equipment of the men is about as good, except for your company of Kentuckians. Chew on that for a spell, and gimme a drink."

Sherman passed over the jug, and Houston lifted it. Suddenly he set it down and leaped to his feet. Shouts were rising through the town and camp. A galloping horse came to a halt outside. Into the headquarters tent burst the scout Karnes, waving a paper. Colonel Austin and other officers followed him in.

"We met up with Mrs. Dickinson twenty mile out," panted Karnes. "Her and a couple negroes—all that's alive out'n the Alamo. Cap'n Dickinson and the kid were killed. Deef Smith stayed to fetch her along in. I come with the news, and this. She got it from General Sesma as she was leaving Bexar—"

HOUSTON SEIZED the paper—a boasting proclamation signed by Santa Anna and ordering death and no quarter to all rebels.

"Well, Karnes? What news?"

"It's all true," groaned the scout. "Every last one dead. Nobody surrendered. And Santy Anny's got thousands and thousands of men, she says. He didn't even bury the bodies, but burned 'em. And he's got another army as big under Gin'ral Urrea who's grabbed Fannin and Goliad by this time. He's a-sweeping all Texas, and she heard some talk that he's a-going right on into the States as well."

So the news of the Alamo was poured forth, while Houston stood with shaggy brows knit and resolve hardening within him. A few hundred men should have gathered at San Felipe by this time, with provisions, powder and stores. He beckoned his aid, Colonel Austin, aside.

"Ride like hell for San Felipe, Bill. I got to stick right here and—what's that, Karnes? What was that last?"

"She says Santy Anny's coming right on, may be here any time," said Karnes. "He aims to burn every house and kill every settler that ain't Mexican by birth. And he's on the way."

"Well, shut your damned mouth about it," snapped Houston, but it was too late now. With an oath, he turned back to Austin. "You see? Now I got to bring off all these here settlers and fight off the Mexicans, if they're coming. Get to San Felipe. Raise every man you can, get powder and transport and cannon somehow! Drill those men if you get a chance. For God's sake check any panic, Bill!"

Austin nodded and departed.

Later, Mrs. Dickinson and the two negroes were brought in. Deaf Smith, the famous scout, came straight to Houston with one of the negroes, who had been the slave of Travis. Houston learned the details, then asked after Mrs. Dickinson.

"Some o' them women are takin' care of her," said Smith. "She's goin' to have a baby pretty soon and she's downright hysterical. She'll raise hell, lemme tell you, Sam."

And she did, poor soul. True, General Sesma was coming with a mere seven hundred dragoons; but Mrs. Dickinson's nerve-shattered fears magnified this into thousands. Neither Houston nor anyone else had definite information on the numbers of Santa Anna's army. It was certainly composed of two or three columns aiming to sweep all Texas, and it was most assuredly some thousands strong, with artillery, lancers and dragoons.

PANIC SEIZED upon Gonzales and upon the army here. The one thought was of flight, and Houston could barely impose some semblance of order on that flight. His own men were deserting hourly, rushing away to get their families and friends out of the tornado's path. These deserters, galloping from town to town, spread wild stories, which grew more wild as they were handed on. Throughout eastern Texas the panic became universal. Every man's intent was now to get his own family to safety, regardless. Every community had but the one thought— to protect its own women and children. Consequently, all thought of joining the army was abandoned. Let others do that! And none did.

Gonzales was abandoned and burned. Slowly, Houston retreated, gathering in all the settlers as he went, protecting the
flood of refugees that poured across the wide plains. He sent
out frantically for reinforcements and aid. The men from San
Felipe joined him and raised his force to six hundred in all. Two
cannon were promised, but came not.

So at last he came to the Colorado River of Texas, crossed
it, and halted. Various skirmishes had temporarily checked the
Mexicans, who were now awaiting their main columns. They
were across the river, almost within sight. And here began Sam
Houston's weeks of agony, as he devoted himself to drilling his
men and keeping them in hand, hoping against hope that
Fannin might yet join him.

The few hundred men under his command were the whole
hope of Texas. What these men wanted was to fight—and do
it now.

Harsh, uncompromising, blunt as ever, he refused flatly to
jeopardize Texas until he got artillery, powder, men and food.
Rations were scant. Daily Houston looked for word of relief,
but his emissaries returned empty-handed. And Santa Anna
was advancing, with artillery.

Houston's men jeered at him to his face, hotly telling him
that rifles alone would send the Mexicans flying. They begged
with him, pleaded with him, swore at him; he remained adamant.
President Burnet and the new government, at San Felipe, were
moving heaven and earth to raise men and money and guns.
Food was coming; let the army wait until it came, with the
cannon.

No use. They wore him down, actual mutiny threatened, his
authority evaporated. Six hundred men could whip all Mexico!
Sherman told him frankly that the men could no longer be
controlled, and for his own sake he must yield. So, bitter-
hearted, he yielded. It was arranged that on the following
morning, the army should cross the river and attack the Mexican
camp hand to hand. Details were set forth—and then, suddenly, a scout came in with news.

Johnson's force had been destroyed. Ward had capitulated. Fannin's entire force was captured and massacred—the first definite news of this. And columns of the enemy were pouring forward in overwhelming numbers.

The army was stunned, paralyzed. All thought of attack was given over. Vainly did Houston pronounce the news false—men knew better. The delusion that Texians could not be defeated was gone. Suddenly all the army realized its own weakness.

Next day came further news, and the darkness began indeed to clamp down on Sam Houston. The cabinet, the whole Texan government, was in flight. San Felipe was being abandoned; New Washington, named as the capital, was being abandoned. East to Harrisburg for the government of republican Texas! Harrisburg and safety!

Sam Houston swore heartily and sat him down to write his steadfast friend Rusk, the secretary of war:

> *"You know I am not easily depressed, but before God I swear that since we parted I have found the darkest hours of my life. For two days and nights I have not eaten an ounce of anything, or slept for a moment...."*

RETREAT NOW, retreat once more. Another flood of frightened settlers to be moved back eastward. Back to San Felipe on the Brazos River—a nightmare march with pitiless cold and rain, with the Mexican dragoons pressing close behind, and a flooded river ahead to cross. It was crossed at last and the bridge destroyed. Another respite now, a chance to hope and breathe.

Vituperation poured upon Houston from every side. What! Run away from these Mexicans? Let them burn and slay on every side without hindrance? Sam Houston was only a lawyer after all. He knew nothing about fighting. He was ruining Texas.

The army murmured. Houston was drilling them day and night, preparing them to meet artillery, cavalry, trained infantry; teaching them to obey orders. Who was he to give them orders anyhow? By God, they were just as good as Sam Houston any day! And they'd prove it. They'd elect another general. Why, he didn't even consult with them or with the officers about what to do! True enough.

"I hold no councils of war," Houston wrote the government. "If I err, the blame is mine."

He drilled them himself, and they hated him for it; but they dared not defy him to his face. The power was there, in those deep gray eyes; the spirit was there, the courage of endurance, the domination that comes from suffering and patience. The one man on whom he could rely utterly was Deaf Smith, the scout, who came and went. Santa Anna was at San Felipe now. If he crossed the Brazos, all was lost. Captain Baker with a handful of men was holding the ford there against him.

One night, without warning, Deaf Smith showed up.

"Fighting," he reported curtly. "Baker's held the ford two days and repulsed Santy Anny, Gin-ral."

"Thank God," breathed Houston. "Sure of it, Deef?"

"Yeah, but that ain't all, Sam. He's got acrost at Thompson's Ferry and is heading for Harrisburg with the hull damned army after him."

"What!" Houston leaped up. "For Harrisburg? But—"

"Ain't no buts, Sam. The president and the cabinet's done skipped out for Galveston. I met up with Rusk, the sec'etery of war, down the road; he's headin' to join up with you. Got a few fellers with him."

Houston sank down on his camp stool, and swallowed hard. "I suppose you don't know anything about how many men Santa Anna has? Or if he's heading down the Brazos—why, he'd have to do that, to reach Harrisburg!"

"He sure is. Got about a thousand men with him. The rest of his army is in two other columns. Sam, one north, one south—hey! What's up?"

For, with one bound, Houston was out of his seat, a flame in his gray eyes.

"Are you sure? Sure? Careful now, Deef! Sure of those numbers?"

"Yeah. We done caught a feller from his column."

"Thank God; oh, thank God!" cried Houston, and grabbed his hat. "Go get some sleep, Deef. We're marching in the morning. See you later."

NO SLEEP for Sam Houston this night. When Rusk showed up, Houston grappled him in a bearlike embrace. A courier came dashing in, as the army was turning out hastily, with a letter from the acting secretary, who had taken the place of Rusk. A letter of bitter vituperation, demanding action from Houston; a frightened, panicky letter. And the government had fled to Galveston! Houston grinned and tucked the script away.

"We're marching in the morning, boys. Get ready," boomed out Houston's voice as the torches flung red radiance on his bronzed features, no longer weary. "Five hundred and twenty-five men, huh? That's enough, I reckon. You'll get your bellies full o' fight this trip, boys! Dismissed."

Yells of glee, sudden vociferous shouts for Sam Houston. New shouts rang forth, new yells pealed up. Into camp past the sentries slogged a wagon, then another. Two six-pounders, sent by friends of Texas from Cincinnati—here in the nick of time! The packing cases still unopened.

Houston detailed artillery men to get the guns assembled, saw to every detail of preparation himself, came back to head-quarters dead tired. There he found Deaf Smith.

"I got me enough sleep, Sam," said the scout. "Let's get busy. Need me?"

"We sure do, Deef. Take all the scouts you can find, and trail Santa Anna's column. If he's heading for Harrisburg, he's bound to cross the river at the Lynchburg ferry. I'll get there first—and if I do, we've got him where we want him! Have word for me sure. We'll set out at daylight, and by next morning ought to be there."

"Got you. Good luck, Sam," and Deaf Smith was gone.

Dead tired as he was, Sam Houston sat gazing into the flame of his candle for a long while before turning in. Suddenly, unexpectedly, he saw the one thing he had prayed heaven to grant him coming true—a chance to smash at the head and center of the whole Mexican army. A thousand men; no more than two to his one. And two cannon had come. It was his hour, his hour, and the hour of Texas!

No haphazard. No mere chance. He saw the thing clearly. From this moment he planned the event. Nothing should spoil his stroke now; whatever happened, he must go through with it as he saw it.

That resolve was to be tested sorely.

Santa Anna would reach Harrisburg, yes; but coming back, he must cross by Lynch's Ferry. Santa Anna, with a thousand men, away from the main body of his army which was sweeping over the whole country! Sam Houston went to bed with ringing thoughts.

Daybreak found him up and off—the last march.

SANTA ANNA not only reached Harrisburg, but burned it. He tried to catch the Texas government, and was within five minutes of bagging the whole crowd from the president down. He took New Washington unhindered, then turned from Galveston Bay and headed through the oaks and brush for Lynch's Ferry. He had no suspicion that Sam Houston was ahead of him.

Ahead of him, yes; and Deaf Smith was on the job. After that long and weary march, the Texas army was worn out. The Mexican vanguard came up. Houston steadily declined battle, ordered his men to eat and sleep. The Cincinnati cannon, the "Twin Sisters," were in battery. The camp was fortified.

Santa Anna described the little camp, with its gaily waving flag bearing the figure of Liberty, and laughed. Grimly calm as any Indian, Sam Houston watched the Mexican forces encamp. He had chosen the position to suit himself, and he meant to choose the time to suit himself also—that was part of his plan.

He did not intend to throw his men into battle directly after a march.

When the Mexican cannon opened, however, and their skirmishers, that afternoon, crept forward under cover, he had them cleared out in short order. The "Twin Sisters" opened fire, his horsemen charged, and the skirmish was over. Late that night, Deaf Smith came into Houston's tent and wakened him.

"Hey, Sam! I didn't want to blurt it out afore anybody, but there's a hell of a lot o' Mexicans on the way. They ain't far, neither. Gin'ral Cos and his dragoons."

Houston caught his breath, then assented calmly.

"Thanks, Deef. You stick around; be here at daylight sure. I got work for you."

No more sleep that night. General Cos and more dragoons! How many? Hard to say. Yet the plan must hold at all costs. Regardless of odds. So Santa Anna did not attack because he was waiting for Cos, eh? Sly fellow, that El Presidente!

Daylight. Houston took Deaf Smith into his tent and showed him a number of axes.

"Deef, pick your own men and get to work. Suppose anything happened so's those Mexicans wanted to get away from here in a hurry. How'd they get over the San Jacinto?"

"They might swim," said Deaf Smith, with a grin. "Or they might cross by Vince's bridge, down the stream a ways. That's how they got here."

"You go cut away Vince's bridge, then," said Houston. "And get back here in a hurry if you want to see the fun."

No mean job, this; several miles of woods to cross, and a bridge to cut, while the Mexicans were all about. Deaf Smith set forth with his party, but on learning their objective they balked flatly. Moses Lapham alone went on with him, and Vince's bridge was destroyed—not before General Cos and five hundred men rode over it, however.

MORNING PASSED. Toward noon, Cos and the dragoons were espied, riding in to swell the force of Santa Anna. Houston roared as his men pointed them out, roared with laughter.

"Why, you fools, Santa Anna's marching some of his men out, around a swell of the prairie, and back in sight of us—to make us think he's getting reinforcements."

None the less, uneasiness reigned through the camp. Houston had his scouts out, obtained precise and rapid reports, knew exactly what he was doing. Halfway between the two camps was a large grove of timber—and upon this point, Sam Houston was preparing his whole stroke.

Noon came. By this time, the certain news that General Cos had arrived could no longer be disguised. What with one party and another coming in, Houston now had seven hundred men. He knew very well that Santa Anna had twice his number. And now, almost at the last moment, a new disaster threatened his whole plan.

His officers, backed by their men, demanded that he hold a council of war.

"All right, boys," and Houston chuckled. "Come right ahead and we'll hold it. But remember one thing! I'm giving the orders here, and by God, I'll shoot the first man who doesn't obey them—no matter who he is. Come along, all hands!"

The senior officers gathered. Faint heart was ruling again; the army was strongly posted, came the argument, and Santa Anna should be made to attack. That way, the great disparity in numbers would be discounted. Sam Houston said nothing at all, but listened in grim silence. Two officers were for attack. The rest voted them down.

"All right, boys; much obliged," said Houston. "I ain't ready to give any orders yet, so I vote we all have a drink around."

No word yet from Deaf Smith. The afternoon wore on. Three o'clock came and passed. The scouts reported that the Mexican cavalry horses were being watered, that all the army, and the dragoons who had arrived that morning, were taking the usual siesta. Then Deaf Smith slipped into camp. He nodded to Houston. The latter swung around to his officers.

"All right, boys. Let's lick Santa Anna before he gets his boots on. Sherman! Burleson! Millard!"

He gave the orders rapidly. One startled gasp, and they obeyed. The men obeyed. The cavalry under Millard mounted and rode forth, sweeping around openly to the attack of the Mexican left. Meantime, the Texians were massing forward, covered by the heavy timber from sight of the Mexican sentinels.

They burst forth. The Twin Sisters vomited grape into the camp ahead. Houston was with the charge. His voice rang out and led the rippling yell.

"Remember the Alamo! Remember Goliad!"

In wild, hasty alarm, the Mexicans attempted some formation. A ragged fire was opened. Not until the charging Texians were close, did their rifles answer the musketry—then death hailed into the ranks ahead. The dragoons broke and fled. The Mexican muskets were still stacked, to a large extent; the surprise of the moment was complete.

Houston's horse was shot under him. He mounted another, followed his yelling line of men over the breastworks and into the Mexican camp. Here a desperate defense was attempted, but it was crushed almost at once. A sudden agonizing pain, and Houston felt himself going down—ankle smashed and horse killed with the same ball.

Someone lent him a hand. He sat down and surveyed the frightful, incredible scene before him.

IT WAS no longer a battle, but a massacre. The Mexican cavalry had attempted to cross the bayou directly behind the camp, only to find it a hopeless morass; men and horses lay strewn everywhere, forming a causeway over which the Texians advanced in further pursuit. No rifles now. Bayonets and bowie knives alone were doing the work. A horrible wailing sound, the sound of men screaming in death, rose over the field. The Mexican infantry were in panic-stricken flight.

The Texians caught dragoon horses and went in pursuit. Such of the Mexican lancers as could, headed the wild flight for Vince's bridge. The pursuing avengers were close behind them—and there was no bridge. A few swam their horses across the stream, but more died there.

Far and wide, by bayou and prairie and oak-grove, the slaughter spread. No orders could check it; Texas had it coming. It was April 21st. Six weeks before, the Alamo had fallen. A month before, the Goliad butchery had taken place. Here were the men who had done those things, some of them, and the army went mad.

Sam Houston was carried back to his own camp. His wound was excessively painful, but exultation conquered pain. As the afternoon hours passed, his orders began to take effect. The lust of killing passed away, and prisoners dribbled in. By evening, six hundred were gathered together and guards posted.

Jubilation reigned supreme. Discipline was lost; the impossible had been accomplished, and now was the time to celebrate. From Santa Anna's private supplies came wine, champagne, delicacies of all kinds. His private effects were looted. His treasure chest was brought in, with ten thousand dollars in coin, and Sam Houston grinned, when they asked him what to do with it.

"Well, boys, I reckon you-all have earned it! And you ain't had no pay, so—"

Wild whoops went up. Food, liquor, victory! Mexican powder lighted the woods in boyish explosions. Songs were chorused up to the stars. With midnight, order was coming back, and things were got in hand.

MORNING FOUND Sam Houston, at least, clear-headed. Despatches to write, couriers to get off, a million and one arrangements to make, plunder to be gathered—everything to be done, and his ankle smashed. Detachments were sent out to bring in all the prisoners possible. No sign of Santa Anna anywhere among the dead, nor among the captives. Part of the army went off to hunt, for deer were plentiful hereabouts.

The day passed. Toward dusk, two men came riding in with a shabby little fellow they had picked up down the bayou, scared to death and shedding tears. They started to turn him in among the prisoners, and a murmur arose.

"El Presidente! El Presidente!"

Better look into this, said somebody. Might be Santa Anna, even if he does deny it. Take him to the gin'ral.

Sam Houston, snatching brief reprieve from the consuming pain of his smashed ankle, was asleep. When they woke him and told him that Santa Anna had been brought in—well, there is more than one story to that. Whether rough old Sam uttered the famous "mot" of General Cambronne at Waterloo, or whether he made the polite and polished bit of oratory that later history puts into his mouth, may be conjectured.

At all events, when he found that he really had the top prize in his hand, he was wide awake enough. For he, and no one else, realized what this prize could and would mean to Texas—and the utter mad folly that would lie in executing the murderer of Alamo and Goliad.

He sat late into the night, aflame with his vision. He still had seven hundred men, or a few less; and there were still Mexican generals galore, with thousands of picked men and artillery to north and south. There was one man those Mexicans would obey, and one only—the dictator, the President of all Mexico.

"Sit down and write," he muttered. "Sit down and write, *El Presidente*. Send the message to your generals. Tell them to evacuate Texas, and do it now. The alternative will not be pleasant matter for you to face, after Goliad—"

A greater victory there than any battle, if he could pull it off. This one little opium-sodden bit of flesh, whom he could strike out of existence with one hand—and with joy—could mean more to Texas in his abject cowardice than ten thousand men. So Sam Houston sat and dreamed into the night hours.

And his dreams came true.

THE MEN WHO FOUGHT FOR TEXAS

A HUNDRED YEARS is not long in the cycle of time, but it is a long time in the history of Texas, and this year when Texas is celebrating its Hundred Years, much is being written of those fighting days and men are living once more in the past as they read such stirring stories as those which *Short Stories'* favorite H. Bedford-Jones is writing in his *Dead Men Singing.*

"My purpose in these articles," writes Mr. Bedford-Jones, "is to try and paint those fighting Texians as they were, and strip away the trappings of pompous falsehood which have largely surrounded them. In no case have I chosen to mention any of the unfortunate accidents of birth or habit in which many of them were involved. It is no detraction to call them hard drinkers—they lived in a day when liquor flowed like water. We are concerned only with their deeds, and in most cases with their deaths. These men did glorious things, and even to mention any peccadillos of faith or morals would be a scurrilous thing."

H . BEDFORD-JONES

BEDFORD-JONES IS a Canadian by birth, but not by profession, having removed to the United States at the age of one year. For over twenty years he has been more or less profitably engaged in writing and traveling. As he has seldom resided in one place longer than a year or so and is a person of retiring habits, he is somewhat a man of mystery; more than once he has suffered from unscrupulous gentlemen who impersonated him—one of whom murdered a wife and was subsequently shot by the police, luckily after losing his alias.

The real Bedford-Jones is an elderly man, whose gray hair and precise attire give him rather the appearance of a retired foreign diplomat. His hobby is stamp collecting, and his collection of Japan is said to be one of the finest in existence. At present writing he is en route to Morocco, and when this appears in print he will probably be somewhere on the Mojave Desert in company with Erle Stanley Gardner.

Questioned as to the main facts in his life, he declared there was only one main fact, but it was not for publication; that his life had been uneventful except for numerous financial losses, and that his only adventures lay in evading adventurers. In his younger years he was something of an athlete, but the encroachments of age preclude any active pursuits except that of motoring. He is usually to be found poring over his stamps, working at his typewriter, or laboring in his California rose garden, which is one of the sights of Cathedral Cañon, near Palm Springs.

Bedford-Jones has written stories laid in many corners of the earth, but among his most popular tales were the John Solomon stories which started many years ago in the *Argosy*.

www.ingramcontent.com/pod-product-compliance
Lightning Source LLC
Chambersburg PA
CBHW061324200626
46813CB00017B/3050